ANDY STANTON

Natboff!

ONE MILLION YEARS OF STUPIDITY

Illustrated by
David Tazzyman

EGMONT

CONTENTS

PRAISE FOR *Mr Gum*:

'Funny? You bet.' **Guardian**

'Andy Stanton accumulates silliness and jokes in an irresistible, laughter-inducing romp.' Sunday Times

'Raucous, revoltingly rambunctious and nose-snortingly funny.' Daily Mail

'It's hilarious, it's brilliant . . . Stanton's the Guv'nor, The Boss.' Danny Baker, BBC London Radio

'It provoked long and painful belly laughs from my daughter, who is eight.' Daily Telegraph

'They're the funniest books . . . I can't recommend them enough.' Stephen Mangan

'They are brilliant.' Zoe Ball, Radio 2

'Funniest book I have ever and will ever read . . . When I read this to my mum she burst out laughing and nearly wet herself . . . When I had finished the book I wanted to read it all over again it was so good.' Bryony, aged 8

'Do not even think about buying another book – This is gut-spillingly funty.' Alex, aged 13

int.'

ACC. No: 07025449

For Tony McGowan - AS
For Mrs Aubrey - DT

EGMONT

We bring stories to life

First published in Great Britain 2018
by Egmont UK Limited
The Yellow Building, 1 Nicholas Road, London W11 4AN

Text copyright © 2018 Andy Stanton
Illustrations copyright © 2018 David Tazzyman

The moral rights of the author and illustrators have been asserted

978 1 4052 9098 2
68623/001

A CIP catalogue record for this title is available
from the British Library

Typeset by Avon DataSet Ltd, Bidford on Avon, Warwickshire
Printed and bound in Great Britain by the CPI Group

20,000 YEARS BC

NATBOFF

Long long timm go in Lamonic Bibber was cavma days. Bigges cavma was Natboff.

'ME THROW ROCK AT MITY WOOLY MAMMOF!' say Natboff. 'HAHA! WOOLY MAMMOF CRY LIKK BABY! NATBOFF BIG AN STRONG! NATBOFF HARIES FATTES CAVMA OF AL TIMM! NATBOFF BESTT!'

But liff always go rong. Wun day Natboff walkig alonn wen com acros even bigge harier cavma of al timm.

'HOO YOU?' say Natboff.

'ME CHUNKA!' say even bigge cavma.

'NATBOFF HATE CHUNKA!' say Natboff.

'NATBOFF EAT CHUNKA!' say Natboff.

Natboff try eat Chunka but Natboff no gud at. Chunka leg to thik for Natboff teeth.

'HAHA,' say Chunka. 'NATBOFF PATHETI! CHUNKA BESST!

'NATBOFF GOT CAV?' say Chunka.

'YEAH,' say Natboff.

'NATBOFF GOT WIFE?' say Chunka.

'YEAH,' say Natboff.

'WAT WIFE NAME?' say Chunka.

'WIFE NAME SALLY,' say Natboff.

'WEL, THIS CHUNKA LUKKY DAY,' say Chunka. 'NOW CHUNKA COM TO NATBOFF CAV AN STEEL NATBOFF WIFE.'

O NO, thinnk Natboff. *NATBOFF WISH NATBOFF NO TELL CHUNKA ABOU CAV AN WIFE.*

'HEY CHUNKA,' say Natboff, crafty stile. 'YOU KNO JUS NOW WEN NATBOFF TELL YOU ABOU CAV AN WIFE CAL SALLY? NATBOFF WAS ONLEH MAKK JOKKE! THER NO CAV! THER NO SALLY! JUS FUNNEH JOKKE!'

'TO LATE,' say Chunka. 'CHUNKA CAN TEL THEY REAL. CHUNKA COMIG

TO CAV TO STEEL WIFE.'

O NO, thinnk Natboff. *CHUNKA NOT JUS FAT AN HARY. CHUNKA A CLEVA FELLO INTO THE BARGEN.*

Chunka go to Natboff cav an grab up
Sally.

'HEY SALLY,' say Chunka. 'ME
CHUNKA. ME MUCH BETER AN FATTER
AN HARIER THAN NATBOFF. YOU COM
WIV CHUNKA NOW.'

'IT TRUE,' say Sally. 'CHUNKA SO
BIG AN FAT AN HARY! SALLY NO
LOV NATBOFF NO MORE! SALLY LOV
CHUNKA NOW! SALLY AN CHUNKA IN
LOV!'

'HA HA,' say Chunka. 'CHUNKA
DONE IT AGEN!'

Chunka throw roks at Natboff an Sally
spit in Natboff har. Then Chunka an Sally run
way way off into foress to do baby cavmas.

Natboff ver sad. Natboff do cry.

Wolf com along an lick up Natboff tears

fro eyes.

'WOLF BE NATBOFF FREND?' say
Natboff.

Wolf nod.

'WOLF BE NATBOFF WIFE?' say
Natboff hopfuly.

Wolf laff an shak hed.

'BUT WOLF BE NICE TO NATBOFF AT
LEEST?' say Natboff.

Wolf nod.

'MEBBE THINNGS NOT SO BAD
AFTEH AL,' say Natboff.

But at night Wolf eat Natboff!

Now Natboff in Wolf tummy.

'THIS WORST DAY OF NATBOFF
LIFF,' say Natboff. 'WAT NATBOFF DO
NOW?'

Natboff com up wiv plan.

NATBOFF WAIT TIL WOLF NEED TOILET IN BUSH, thinnk Natboff. *THEN NATBOFF COM OUT OF WOLF AGEN! BETER THAN EVEH!*

So Natboff wait al day wile Wolf run round eatig stuf. Lateh on Wolf get belly rumbles.

'O NO,' say Wolf. 'WOLF NEED FIND BUSH BEFOR TO LATE.'

HERE ME CHANSE, thinnk Natboff.

Wolf go to bush an push it al out. Out com Natboff, beter than eveh! (But a bit smel.)

'NEVEH MIN,' say Natboff to himsel. 'STIL GUD TO BE OUT OF WOLF AGEN.'

Natboff go up to Wolf.

'NAUGTY WOLF!' shou Natboff. 'YOU SAY YOU NATBOFF FREND! BUT YOU

EAT NATBOFF!'

'SORY,' say Wolf. 'ME FORGET.'

'OK,' say Natboff. 'BUT YOU NATBOFF FREND NOW?'

'DEFINETT,' say Wolf. 'WOLF AN NATBOFF FREND. WOLF AN NATBOFF DO DISCO TO SELEBRAT.'

So Wolf an Natboff do disco in cav. It fun, but it stil not solv probbem.

'IT FUN, BUT IT STIL NOT SOLV PROBBEM,' say Natboff. 'SALLY STIL WIV CHUNKA. WAT NATBOFF DO NOW?'

'GO ON INTERNET,' say Wolf, 'MEBBE THAT HELP.'

So Natboff go on internet but it cavma days, long long go, an bak then internet jus big rok wiv 'Google' carve on. No help at al!

'INTERNET RUBISH!' say Natboff.

'NATBOFF HATE INTERNET!'

Wolf eat internet.

'NOW WAT NATBOFF DO?' say
Natboff.

'WOLF GET HELP FROM FRENDS,' say
Wolf.

'WOLF GOT MITY FRENDS?' say
Natboff.

'MITIEST EVEH!' say Wolf prowdly.
'WOLF GO AN GET MITY FRENDS. THEN
CHUNKA GOT NO CHANSE!'

Wolf run out of cav.

Natboff wait.

Natboff wait a bit mor.

Natboff wait ages.

Natboff wait Stone Ages.

Natboff discoveh fire.

Natboff happy!

Natboff set har on fire!

Natboff not so happy.

'WOLF TAKIG FOREVEH,' say Natboff.

Natboff starvig.

Natboff eat own burnned har.

'BURNNED HAR DISGUSSIG,' say
Natboff.

Natboff spit har out everwher.

Natboff try eatig cav.

No gud.

Evencherlee Wolf come bak wiv frends.

'LOOK AT MITY FRENDS,' Wolf say
prowdly.

'MITY ANT!

'MITY SPIDA!

'MITY LEEF!'

'FRENDS NOT LOOK SO MITY,'
say Natboff. 'NATBOFF THURT WOLF'S

FRENDS BE MITY BEAR! MITY MAMMOF!
MITY SABE-TOOTH TIGGER!'

'SORY,' say Wolf. 'WOLF NOT KNO
THOSE GUYS. WOLF ONLY KNO MITY
ANT! MITY SPIDA! MITY LEEF!'

'ME CAN DO THIRTY PRES-UPS,' say
Mity Leef.

'OK,' say Natboff. 'IT HAV TO DO. WAT
THE PLAN?'

'CHUNKA LIV IN FORESS WIV SALLY
NOW,' say Mity Spida. 'SO WE GOT TO
GO TO FORESS. THEN WE SNEEK UP ON
CHUNKA.'

'IS GUD START TO PLAN,' say Natboff.
'BUT WAT NEX?'

'MITY ANT JUMP ON CHUNKA
LEGG AN LICK HIM,' say Mity Spida.
'THEN MITY SPIDA (THAT ME) TIKLE

CHUNKA FOOT. THEN WOLF BITE OFF
CHUNKA FACE. NATBOFF GET SALLY
BACK, EESY PEESY LEMMO SQUEE!'

'MITY SPIDA GUD AT PLAN!' say
Natboff. 'MABBE THIS WURK AFTEH AL.
BUT WAT ABOU MITY LEEF? EVERWUN
ELSE DO STUF IN PLAN BUT MITY LEEF
DO NUTHIN.'

'ME DO PRES-UPS TO DISTRAC
CHUNKA,' say Mity Leef, flexig mussels.

'IT GUDDEST PLAN OF AL TIMM!' say
Wolf. 'LET DO DISCO TO SELEBRAT.'

Natboff, Wolf, Mity Ant, Mity Spida an
Mity Leef do disco.

Gess hoo besst at disco dancc? Mity Ant.

Mity Ant win disco prize!

'DISCO FUN,' say Natboff. 'BUT NOW
IT TIMM FOR PUT PLAN INTO ACSHUN.

WICH WAY FORESS?'

Mity Leef step forwar.

'ME WAS BORN IN FORESS,' say Mity
Leef, 'SO ME KNO EXAC WHER IT IS.
FOLLO LEEF!'

'NATBOFF HAD DOUTS ABOU MITY
LEEF TO BEGIN WIV,' say Natboff, 'BUT
NOW HE GROWIG ON ME.'

'HA HA,' say Mity Ant. 'NATBOFF
MAKK BIG FUNNEH!'

'DISCO TO SELEBRAT?' say Wolf
hopfully.

'MABBE LATEH,' say Natboff.

AL WOLF WANT TO DO IS DISCO,
thinnk Natboff. *ME GETTIG PRETTY SICK
OF WOLF. BUT ME NOT TELL WOLF OUT
LOUD BECOS WOLF NATBOFF FREND,
AN ME NOT WANT TO HURT WOLF*

13

FEELIG.

(Natboff mite be cavma but Natboff a sensitif sort of fello.)

Anyweh. Afteh al this, Natboff an gang set off wiv Mity Leef leedig way. Evencherlee com to foress.

Gess hoo in middel of foress tryig to makk baby cavmas? It Chunka an Sally, jus as Natboff susspecced!

'YOU GUYS HIDDE IN BUSH,' say Natboff to anima an plannt chums. 'NATBOFF GONNA DO IT CRAFTY STILE!'

Natboff step forwar crafty stile to wher Chunka an Sally busy tryig to makk baby cavmas.

'HEY CHUNKA, HEY SALLY,' say Natboff.

'HEY NATBOFF,' say Chunka. 'GO AWAY, WE IN THE MIDDEL OF STUF.'

'NATBOFF NOT COM AL THIS WAY TO BE TALK TO LIKK THAT,' say Natboff. 'NATBOFF COM TO GET SALLY BAK.'

'O YEAH?' say Chunka. 'HOW NATBOFF GONNA DO THAT? CHUNKA SO BIG AN HARY, NATBOFF GOT NO CHANSE.'

'NATBOFF GOT CHUMS,' say Natboff.

Natboff giv the secre comman.

Imedialy Mity Leef jump out of bush an do pres-ups.

Chunka can harly beleev eyes!

Wile Chunka distracced by Mity Leef, Mity Ant jump out an lick Chunka legg!

Wile Chunka try to cope wiv that, Mity Spida run up an tikle Chunka foot!

'WAT GOIN ON?' say Chunka.

Then Wolf jump out an bite off Chunka face!

'OW!' say Chunka face from insidde Wolf. 'OK, OK, CHUNKA GIV IN! NATBOFF WIN.'

'SALLY TOTALL SORY FOR GO OFF WIV CHUNKA BEFOR,' say Sally. 'SALLY TOTALL LOV NATBOFF AGEN NOW. NATBOFF NOT AS FAT AN HARY AS CHUNKA – BUT AT LEES NATBOFF GOT A FACE.'

'DISCO TO SELEBRAT?' say Wolf.

'DEFINETT!' say everwun.

Hole gang do disco in foress. Chunka join in wiv disco too, even tho Chunka got no face. It horibel to watch, but gud try from Chunka.

'CHUNKA NOT SUCH A BAD FELLO

AFTEH AL,' say Natboff.

Lateh on Chunka get steped on by Wooly Mammof.

Natboff an Sally bureh Chunka unerneef bush.

Mity Spida dres up as holy prees an say prayer for Chunka.

Everwun cry.

But liff go on.

Natboff an Sally makk baby cavma an gess wat they cal him?

Chunka!

'IT IN MEMORY OF BESST CAVMA HOO EVEH LIV,' say Natboff, an everwun agree.

'AL IN AL IT BEEN GUD DAY,' say Mity Leef. 'WE DONE BRILLIA AVENCHER. PLUS EVERWUN MADD

NEW FRENDS!'

'SALLY TOTALL LOV NATBOFF FOR AL TIMM,' say Sally.

'*EVERWUN* LOV NATBOFF,' say everwun. (Even Natboff say it! Even baby Chunka say it!)

'DISCO TO SELEBRAT?' say Wolf.

'BIGGES DEFINETT EVEH!' say everwun.

ENND

1115 BC

THE MASSIVE GIANT AND THE FLEA

Many hundreds of years ago, when Lamonic Bibber wasn't even really a town yet, just a few huts and a warlock who lived on Boaster's Hill turning turnips into balloons, there lived a massive giant. Now, this giant's name was Gavin and he really was large. His head, right, his head was so big, right, his head was so big that, well, here's the thing, right, his head was sooooo big that, OK, I hope you're ready for this, his head was soooooo ENORMOUS, right, that OK, hold on, his head was sooooooooo massive that it was about the size, are you sure you're ready for this, his head was sooooo vast that – well, to be honest, I don't really know how big his head was.

But his hands, right, his hands were SO UNBELIEVABLY HUGE, so UNBEARABLY, INCREDIBLY COLOSSAL, right, his hands, his hands yeah, OK, fair enough, I don't know how big his hands were either. But what about his feet? Oh my goodness! You see, Gavin the giant's feet – and I do hope you're sitting down to hear this because it really will blow your mind – well, actually I have no idea how big Gavin the giant's feet were either.

I tell you what, can we start again? The story of 'The Massive Giant And The Flea' is amazing and I want to get it exactly right.

THE MASSIVE GIANT AND THE FLEA

Ages ago, much longer ago than you can remember because you're only about seven, Lamonic Bibber was just a few huts and also there was a warlock who I might have mentioned before who lived on Boaster's Hill turning balloons into hats. But the most incredible person in all that land was not just a person but a MASSIVE GIANT and he was called Gavin the giant.

Oh my word, he was enormous! Each one of his eyes was, well, they were just, they were, look, you know what eyes are normally

23

like, don't you? Of course you do, you've seen eyes before. And not only have you *seen* eyes before, but you've actually *got* eyes, haven't you? So you've seen eyes with your own eyes and you know how big they are, more or less, right? Well, the thing about these eyes of Gavin the giant's, this is what you have to understand – the thing about his eyes was, OK, look, I'm not going to lie to you, I have no idea how big Gavin the giant's eyes were, I really haven't got any idea at all. But I bet you're curious to know how big his nose was, aren't you? And if you are, then you're in for an astonishing treat, because Gavin the giant's nose, you see, Gavin the giant's nose was – OK, hold on.

Imagine a normal person's nose is about the size of an apricot, can you imagine that? Let's say that most people have a nose the size of an apricot, that's a good way to start. Now, bearing in mind that a normal person's nose is about the size of one apricot, one single, delicious apricot that you might find down the greengrocer's, or growing on a tree, actually do apricots grow on trees? Or more on bushes? I'm not sure, I know that tomatoes grow on these little kind of plants with stalks on, tomatoes are nice, aren't they?

I like tomatoes.

Anyway, here's the thing: imagine that a normal person's nose is about the size of one apricot (or roughly three cherry tomatoes). Now, by comparison, Gavin the giant's nose was NOT the size of one apricot, it was bigger than that. How much bigger? I don't know.

Let's start again.

THE MASSIVE GIANT AND THE FLEA

Way, way back in the distant past, Lamonic Bibber was just a few huts and a warlock who lived on Boaster's Hill, turning hats into nightingales. Now, I know this is going to surprise some of you but there was a giant who lived in those days, and I bet you can't guess his name, but it was Gavin.

Now, a lot of people, when they first hear about Gavin the giant, like you are doing now – hearing about Gavin the giant for the first time, I mean – a lot of people immediately want to know all the details. They want to know how big his head was, for example. Or how big his hands were. Or his torso, that's quite a popular one. Which is fair enough, but I don't think that's the most amazing thing about Gavin the giant, and I'm not just saying that because I don't know the answers to all those other questions. I think the most important thing is how tall he was *overall*. I mean, at the end of the day, that is what is so impressive about giants, isn't it? How tall they are *overall*. So sit back and strap yourselves in and prepare to be amazed as I tell you how tall Gavin the giant truly was.

Right. Let's say that a normal man is about, I don't know, about as tall as – let's just say, for example, that a normal man is about as tall as a fencepost. (I know some men are slightly shorter than a fencepost, and some other men are slightly taller than a fencepost but let's just

say, on average, that one man is about as tall as one fencepost.) So we can write down the following equation:

ONE MAN = ONE FENCEPOST

Now, of course, the question is this: How tall was Gavin the giant? And we can write down this question as the following equation:

GAVIN THE GIANT = ???

So. Given that a normal man is about as tall as a fencepost, and given that we don't know how tall Gavin the giant was, it is clear that Gavin the giant was quite a mysterious sort of a character. OK, so we – OK, I tell you what, this has all been a bit confusing what with all these equations and things, let's start again.

THE MASSIVE GIANT AND THE FLEA

Once upon a time there lived a giant called Gavin and one day he saw a flea.

THE END

Bibbering Through The Ages
The Stone Table

The Stone Table that stands on the outskirts of Lamonic Bibber is a mysterious and powerful object of ancient times. Recent tests have revealed that it may be much older than previously thought, perhaps dating as far back as 400 years BC (Before Chairs). Although no one knows exactly what it was used for, it was probably built by the so-called 'Oakic people', a group of nature-worshipping weirdies who spent their time dancing around hillsides, dressed as acorns and singing songs about dead badgers. Today the Oakic people have mostly been forgotten, although some of their rites and ceremonies have survived into the modern age, such as the Festival of the Leaves, which still takes place every autumn, and the Eurovision Song Contest, which falls around May. (Thankfully, a number of their *other* ceremonies, such as the Month of Human Sacrifices, the Other Month of Human Sacrifices, and the notorious 'Nudey Day', have died out naturally over time.)

Once Upon a Time . . .

Princess Snowflake and the Gypsy King

Once upon a time, long ago in the Age of Fairy Tales, when the whole wide world was sugar and spice and apples and mice and snow and ice and moonbeams, there lived in Lamonic Bibber a princess called Princess Snowflake. And never was there a name more suited to a person, because for a start she was a princess, so that bit was definitely right. And also she looked a bit like a snowflake, for her face was pale as a December's morning and her hair as silver as light reflecting off snow. And finally, she was every bit as wild and carefree as a snowflake, so there you have it. Princess Snowflake it was.

Princess Snowflake's parents had mysteriously disappeared soon after she was born, and so it was that a bunch of kindly old witches had agreed to raise the child as their own. They lived with her in the Winter Palace, which was made entirely of ice. The chambers, the towers, even the door handles – everything was made of ice. The floors were a bit slippery, and it was best to put a blanket on the seat before you went to the toilet, but it was still a palace, so never mind.

On the whole, Princess Snowflake led a carefree life, as I have said. But one day, when she was five years old, one of the kindly old witches took her aside.

'Child,' said the witch. 'I have something important to tell you. You know the Winter Gardens, which lie beyond the palace walls? Well, they are very nice. But take heed, for a dreadful fellow lurks deep within those gardens, waiting to trap the unwary! It is the Gypsy King, and he is strong, with rippling muscles, and he wears hundreds of gold rings on his fingers, and he has proud boots. Beware the Gypsy King, child, beware the Gypsy King!'

But Princess Snowflake only clapped her hands together, one, two, three!

'Gypsy King?' she laughed. 'There's no such thing as the Gypsy King! I don't need your help, I don't need anyone's help!'

And off she ran to explore the gardens, for they were her greatest joy.

When Princess Snowflake was six years old, another of the kindly old witches took her aside.

'Uh oh,' said Princess Snowflake, 'here we go again.'

'Child,' said the kindly old witch. 'You know the Winter Gardens? Well, they are very nice. But from time to time they are visited by one who seeks to harm the unwary! Yes, it is the Gypsy King, and he is strong, with rippling muscles, and he wears hundreds of gold rings on his fingers, and he has proud boots.'

But Princess Snowflake only clapped her hands together, one, two, three!

'There's no such thing as the Gypsy King!' she laughed. 'I don't need your help, I don't need anyone's help!'

And off she went to raid the kitchens for her favourite cakes – marzipan disobediences. She didn't like how they tasted, she just liked the name. Princess Snowflake stuffed herself silly with marzipan disobedience cakes, and off she ran to explore the gardens once more.

When Princess Snowflake was seven years old, another of the kindly old witches took her aside.

'Child,' said the kindly old witch. 'You know the –'

But Princess Snowflake only clapped her hands together, one, two, three!

'Yeah, yeah, I've heard it all before,' she said. 'King of the Pixies or something, nasty bloke, don't go near him, blah blah blah. I don't need your help, I don't need anyone's help!'

And off she ran to explore the gardens, slipping on the icy floor and almost colliding with a little hedgehog called Chomley.

With each passing year Princess Snowflake grew more reckless, wandering further and further into the gardens to explore. The witches despaired, but there was nothing to be done and in the end, they gave up even trying to keep her indoors. 'For she has a mind of her own, that girl,' said one. 'Which is fine, it's just that sometimes it's quite an *annoying* mind.'

One day shortly after her eleventh birthday, Princess Snowflake was exploring a part of the gardens she hadn't been in before, her faithful spaniel, Gooseberry, at her side. Merrily she skipped along, scoffing her marzipan disobediences, Chomley the hedgehog racing after her to guzzle up the scraps.

Oh, how beautiful the gardens were! Waxy green holly bushes lined the pathways, so that it always felt like Christmas. Thick pines and fir trees rose all around, like something from a picture book, and the flowerbeds were bursting with every sort of winter plant and herb imaginable: snowdrops and white pansies; snapdragons and turkeybane; Shoveller's Delight and puff-puff-mcguffs; inside-out Nigels, wizard-foot, beards of Persia, frogleytumps, moth-whipper – and many more besides. Everything sparkled with a layer of diamond-dusty white, and the only sounds were the crunching of the snow underfoot and the soft breeze whispering in the branches.

At length, Princess Snowflake came to a little wooden bench set back from the path, and there she sat herself down to watch the world go by. The witches had put up signs all around the bench, saying:

BEWARE THE GYPSY KING!

and

DANGER! THE GYPSY KING IS KNOWN TO OPERATE IN THESE PARTS!

and

YOU'RE GOING TO REGRET NOT READING THESE SIGNS ONE OF THESE DAYS, YOUNG LADY, IN FACT I BET YOU'RE NOT EVEN READING THIS ONE RIGHT NOW, ARE YOU?

'No, I'm not,' said Princess Snowflake, which was true, because she wasn't.

Presently a deer
bounded by with a big 'D'
painted on its side. Then
another one with an
'A'. Then another, with
an 'N'. Then another,
with a 'G'. Then
another, with an 'E'. And then
one more, with an 'R' painted
on its side.

'Oh, how
adorable,' laughed Princess
Snowflake, clapping her
hands together, one, two,
three! 'Those letters must be
the initials of each deer's name! I
bet they are called Daniel, Arthur,
Neil, Georgina, Eleanor and Rum-

Pum-Pum! Rum-Pum-Pum is my
favourite!'

While Princess Snowflake
had been sitting on the bench,
she had let Gooseberry off
his leash so that he could
go and do his business in
the bushes. (Gooseberry
ran a small and very
profitable furniture business
in the undergrowth,
selling small
tables and chairs
and suchlike to the
other animals.
Chomley the hedgehog
was one of his best
customers.)

41

'Gooseberry!' called Princess Snowflake at length. 'Finish up your business and come and walk with me some more, there's a good doggie!'

But no, there *wasn't* a good doggie, because Gooseberry did not come rushing out of the bushes as he normally did, barking and smiling and with dozens of silver coins spilling from his mouth. Gooseberry was nowhere to be seen, and for the first time in her young life, Princess Snowflake knew what it was to feel fear. For the first time, she began to wish that she had listened to the witches. How long had Gooseberry been gone? Ten minutes? An hour? Even as Princess Snowflake rose from the bench to search for him, the day darkened and a cold, crisp flurry of snow began to fall. And as the snow fell, it sang:

Whisper, whisper so,
The wind and the snow
The Gypsy King
And his golden ring
Woe, woe, woe!

Whisper, whisper so,
The frostbite on your toe
The Gypsy King
Will only bring
Woe, woe, woe!

Whisper, whisper so,
The frozen ground below
The Gypsy King
In the fairy ring
Woe, woe, woe!

'What do you mean by this sinister and quite catchy rhyme?' pleaded Princess Snowflake – but the snow would say no more.

For a moment the world stood still.

And then, suddenly, the Gypsy King jumped out from behind a tree. He was strong, with rippling muscles, and he wore hundreds of gold rings on his fingers, and he had proud boots. And in his huge cruel hands he held Princess Snowflake's darling companion, Gooseberry.

'I've done it again,' laughed the Gypsy King. 'All the legends about me were true, I live in the gardens and I snatch up spaniels and do what I like.'

'I hate you,' said Princess Snowflake, throwing herself to the ground and weeping hot, bitter tears that melted the snow all around her. 'What do you want with Gooseberry? He is

only a spaniel and part-time furniture salesman!
But he means more to me than all my riches
put together! Please, please! I will give you all
the land of the town – from the Lamonic River
to Boaster's Hill! From the Stone Table to the
Forest of Runtus! From the meanest hovel to
the Winter Palace itself – it will all be yours,
if you will only return Gooseberry to me, you
unbearable devil!'

But the Gypsy King merely laughed and
put Gooseberry's face to his lips. Then he kissed
Gooseberry's little face, once, twice, three times!
And all at once Gooseberry was gone. But around
the Gypsy King's neck hung a chain that hadn't
been there a moment before. From the chain
dangled a single glass bead, and inside the glass
bead, tiny as a fingernail, was poor Gooseberry.

'That was a bit uncalled-for,' said Princess

Snowflake indignantly.
But the Gypsy King merely threw back his head and laughed once more.

'HA HAHAAHA AHA AHA HAAH
AHAHAHA HAHA AH AH AHHAHAHAH
AH AHAHAH AHA HA HA HA HA
HAHAHA HHA AH AHA HA AH AHA
HAHA HA AH AH AHAH HA HA AH
AHHA AH AHHA HA HA AH AHAHAHAH
AHAHAHAHA AH AHAH AHA HAAHAHA
AHHAHAAH AHAHA AH AHA HA HAAH
HAHAHA AH AHA AHA HAHA HA HA
HAHA AHA HAHA AH HA HA HA HAH
AH AHA HA HAH AHAHA HAAH A AHA
AHA HA HAHAHAHAHA HA HAHAHA
HAH AHH AH AHAHA HAH AHAHA HAH
AHAHAH AHA HA HAHAHAH AHHA
HA AHHA HAHAH AHAH HAHAH AH
AHH AHAH AH AHA HAH HAHAH AHA
HAHAH HA HAH AH AH AHAH AA HAH
AH A AHA HA AHA HA HAHAHA HA

47

HAHAH A HAH HAHAHA HA HAH AHA
HA HA HAH AH AH AHAH AH AH HAH
AH HAHAH AHHAHAHA HAHHAHAHAH
AH HAHAHAHAHA AH AHA HAH A
AHAHAH A HAH AHHAHA AHA HHA
AHAH AHA HAHAAH AH AHAHA HA
AHAH AHHAHAHAHA AHAHAHAHA
HAH AH AHAAH AHA HAHAHA AH
HAH HAHA HAHAHHA AHAHA HAH
AHHAHA HAHAHA HA HAH AHAHAH
AHA HHAHAHAHAHAHAHAH AH AH A
HA HAAHAHAHAHAHAH HAAHA H AH
AH HA HA H AHH AH AH HAHA H AHH
AHHAHA H AH HAHAHHA HA H AH HA
HAHAHHAHAHAHHAHAHAHAHHAHA
H HA HA HA H HA HA A HAA AHA HA AH
AH AHAHA AHH AH A AH AH AH HA HA
HA HA HA HA HA HA AHAHAH AHA HA

HA HAHAHAHHAHAHAHHAHAHAHAH
AHHAHAHAHHAHAH AH HAH AH
AHAHHAHAHAHAHAH AH HA HAHA HA
AHA A HAHA AH AHAHAHAHAH A AHA
AHAHA AHAHA AHAHA AHA A HAHA
HA HAHAHAHA HA AHA HAHA AHA HA
AHAHAH AHA HAHA HA AHA A HA AHAH
AHA AH AHAHHA HA HA HA HA HA HA
HAHAH HAA HAHA AHA H A A AHAHAH
AHA HAHAHAHA HAHAHAHAH HA
AHA AHA AHA AHAHAHAHAHA HA
AHA AHA AHA AHA AHA AHA HA AHA
AH AHA H HA HAHAHA HA HA HAHAH
HA HA HAHA HA AHAHAHAHAHA HA
AHA AHA H HAAAHAAHAHAH H AH
AHAHAHAHHAHAH AHAHAHA AHAH
AHA AH H H H H HA AHA HA AHA HA
AHAHA HA HA HAHAHA HA AHA HA HA,'

laughed the Gypsy King.

Actually the Gypsy King laughed quite a lot more than that, I only wrote a tiny bit of it. All told, he stood there laughing for over six hours, and Princess Snowflake could do nothing but look on helplessly, because she kept thinking, *Surely it's got to end soon, no one can laugh for this long, I'll say something to him in a minute. When he's stopped laughing.* But it just went on and on.

Eventually, just as Princess Snowflake had made up her mind that enough was enough and she was about to tell him off for laughing so much and wasting paper, the Gypsy King turned, his cloak sweeping out behind him – and in a flash he had vanished, just as if he had never been there at all.

Poor Princess Snowflake. She was so distraught that as soon as she got back to the Winter Palace, she took to her icy bed and lay there with her face buried in the pillow, and none of the kindly old witches could rouse her. All that evening they knocked upon her chamber door, singing:

Let us in, let us in
Princess, dearie, let us in
For tho' this life is full of sin
And trouble,
Princess, dearie, let us in

But Princess Snowflake cried, 'Leave me to my sorrows! Begone from my chamber door!'

That night she dreamed a terrible dream. The Gypsy King was standing on a black rock amidst a great lake of fire, untroubled by the flames that licked at his boots and laughing with pure scorn. All about fell thousands and thousands of glass snowflakes, and in each one Princess Snowflake saw Gooseberry's unhappy face. But when she tried to catch one of the snowflakes it slipped through her fingers like sand.

'HA HA AHA HAHAHHAHA!' laughed the Gypsy King. 'You will never get your little dog back, unless you know the thing that I am most afraid of in the world!'

The next evening, the kindly old witches came again to Princess Snowflake's door, singing:

Let us in, let us in
Princess, darling, let us in
For we are here to help in times
Of trouble
Princess, darling, let us in

But again Princess Snowflake cried, 'Begone from my chamber door! Leave me to my miseries!'

Once more she fell into a troubled sleep, and once more she dreamed of the Gypsy King, standing on his black rock amidst the lake of fire. And once more he laughed and said, 'You will never know the thing I am most afraid of in the world! Someone like *you* could never know that!'

On the third evening the witches came again to Princess Snowflake's door, singing:

Let us in, let us in
Princess, sweetheart, let us in
For when the going's hard
And full of trouble –

But this time Princess Snowflake flung the door open wide and she fell to her knees sobbing and begging for forgiveness.

'I told you she'd open the door on the third night,' whispered one of the witches at the back. 'Things always happen in threes in fairy tales. That's a fiver you owe me, Liz.'

'So you do have need of our help after all?' asked the leader of the kindly old witches, who was called Cobwep, because her parents hadn't known how to spell 'Cobweb'.

'Yes, yes!' sobbed Princess Snowflake. 'I have been an impossible child! But I can bear it no longer! Please help me, though I hardly deserve it!'

'It is well spoken,' said Cobwep. 'Sleep now, Princess Snowflake, and we shall return tomorrow evening.'

Gently, Cobwep tucked the child into bed and kissed her goodnight. Princess Snowflake fell asleep with a smile on her face and this time, when she saw the Gypsy King in her dream, he shrank back and cried, 'What! You have protected yourself with the thing I am most afraid of in the world! I hate you, you're stupid!' And he disappeared beneath the flames.

When the witches came back the next evening, they didn't even have to bother coming up with another verse, for the chamber door was open to receive them.

'We have returned to help you, as we said we would,' said Cobwep.

'Thank you, Grandmother,' said Princess Snowflake. (It didn't mean that Cobwep was actually her real grandmother, it is just what children always call old women in fairy tales, no one knows why.) 'Can you ever forgive me for being so awful?'

'Of course, child,' said Cobwep. 'For we only want to see you happy.'

'Then will you . . . Will you help me get Gooseberry back?' asked Princess Snowflake. 'I am so lonely without him.'

'We shall do what we can,' said Cobwep. 'But getting him back will not be easy. You must travel to the Realm of the Gypsy King, and you must travel alone. Are you ready to make the journey?'

'I am,' replied Princess Snowflake.

'Then I shall tell you the way,' said Cobwep, her face wavering in the candlelight like an old flannel. 'You must go into the gardens at midnight, child, when the moon is fat and full.'

'OK,' said Princess Snowflake.

'And you must stick your tongue out, and you must eat the first snowflake that lands on your tongue,' said Cobwep.

'OK,' said Princess Snowflake.

'And then,' said Cobwep, 'you must stick your tongue out a second time, and you must eat the next snowflake that lands on your tongue.'

'OK,' said Princess Snowflake.

'And then,' said Cobwep, 'you must stick your tongue out a third time, and you must eat one last snowflake.'

'OK,' said Princess Snowflake.

'And then,' said Cobwep, 'you must go up to the fir tree, child, the one that stands in the very middle of the gardens, where all the paths meet. And you must eat it.'

'OK,' said Princess Snowflake, 'that's – no, sorry, actually, hold on a minute. What do you mean?'

'Just what I say,' said Cobwep. 'You go up to the fir tree, you open your mouth and you eat it.'

'Let me get this straight,' said Princess Snowflake. 'You want me to eat a fir tree?'

'Yes,' said all the witches together.

'An entire fir tree?'

'Yes,' said the witches.

'Can you do a spell to make it easier, Grandmother?' said Princess Snowflake. 'I mean, I actually know the tree you're talking about, it's – there's no way, I mean – it's . . .

Look, I'm not trying to be ungrateful but – it's, really, it's just – honestly, there's just no way.'

'Sorry, you'll have to manage on your own,' said Cobwep. 'Anyway, we've got to go now, there's another princess in trouble in Russia. She's had her face stolen by ghosts.'

'What, are you going to make *her* eat a fir tree too?' shouted Princess Snowflake. 'I can't believe this is happening, seriously, what on earth are you all thinking.'

'Bye bye, dearie,' said the witches as they left to catch their aeroplane, which was an enormous broomstick driven by a cat. 'You know what to do, good luck.'

Princess Snowflake lay awake until it was midnight. Then, hardly daring to think about the task ahead, out she crept in her nightgown, into the moonlit gardens of the Winter Palace.

The night was deathly quiet and the snow was falling soft and thick.

Princess Snowflake stuck out her tongue and swallowed the first snowflake that landed upon it.

Then she swallowed the second snowflake.

Then she swallowed the third snowflake.

Then she went up to the fir tree which stood in the middle of the gardens where all the paths met, and she started eating it.

'This is a complete nightmare,' sobbed Princess Snowflake as she sat there chewing on a mouthful of bark. 'It's going to take *forever*.'

But each time she wanted to give up, she thought of Gooseberry's innocent little face and she remembered how much the witches loved her and she told herself, 'One more bite, just one more bite.' So the hours passed, though every minute felt like a lifetime.

One more bite, just one more bite . . . And as the night turned to morning and the sun was rising over the gardens, Princess Snowflake realised that the entire fir tree was gone. So it just goes to show: you can do anything if only you believe in yourself. You can win the Olympics. You can become a professor. You can even eat a fir tree. You probably shouldn't eat a fir tree unless you're a princess in a fairy tale. Or a monster. Or a really big woodpecker. But you can if you like. But you shouldn't. But you can if you like. But don't.

As soon as Princess Snowflake had finished the last piece of bark, a glowing line appeared on the ground. Princess Snowflake took a deep breath and coughed up a few fir needles. Then, mustering all her courage, she stepped across the line and as she did so, the gardens of the Winter Palace disappeared and she found herself in the Realm of the Gypsy King. The earth beneath her feet was cracked and dry. A scorching wind blew. And there before her, standing on a black rock surrounded by a lake of fire, stood the Gypsy King himself.

'So!' laughed the Gypsy King. 'You have made it to my Realm, I bet you had to eat a fir tree or something, didn't you? But the rules of this place are not like your world, you fool! Come and get me now, if you dare! But if you cannot defeat me, you shall be trapped here forever! AHA AH AAH AAHAHAHA HAAH AHAA HAAHHAAHAH AHA AHAHA!'

This time the Gypsy King went on laughing for nearly twelve hours, so I definitely won't write it all out. Princess Snowflake waited patiently until the laughter was over and then she said, 'Gypsy King, I care not for your atrocious lake of fire. For I have seen you in my dreams and now I know the thing you are most afraid of in the world.'

And she held out her hands and stood there with her palms open and empty.

'Oh, no,' said the Gypsy King sarcastically. '*Hands*! Oh, no! N . . . Not h-h-*hands*! Oooh, no, I'm *terrified*, oh no, oh, no! Oh, no! The *hands* are going to get me, oh, no! Not the *hands*!'

'Oh, Gypsy King,' said Princess Snowflake. 'It is not the hands themselves, but what they represent. Ever since I was a baby, those around me have worked to protect me and keep me from harm. I never used to listen to them for I was arrogant. But when I threw open my chamber door to let my friends inside, I also threw open the door to my heart. Behold, Gypsy King, for I have finally discovered the thing in the world you are most afraid of – THE POWER OF FRIENDSHIP AND HELPING EACH OTHER.'

At these words, Princess Snowflake's hands were empty no longer, for in her left was clasped the right hand of Cobwep. And in Princess Snowflake's right hand was clasped the left hand of Cobwep's sister, Nightshadf. And then suddenly, there they all were – a vast army of kindly old witches, hands linked together as one, encircling the lake of fire in a chain of true friendship.

Princess Snowflake recognised some of the faces, like Cobwep, and another one called Granny Champion and another one called Roller Jane, who was one of the fattest witches ever born. But there were plenty of others she'd never met before, many thousands and thousands of them, and each one looking upon the Gypsy King with a mixture of pity and compassion which the cruel man could not bear. And now, as one, they started for him across the lake. And the flames weren't even burning them because they were totally magic.

'NO!' shouted the Gypsy King, reaching for Cobwep and meaning to grind her to dust in his golden-ringed hands. But his brute force was no match for the witches' kindliness. Slowly, slowly they closed in, throwing their arms around him and hugging him tight, tight as can be – and he was overcome. Down he went, down, down into the fray as the witches sort of beat him up with their deadly love and hugs and friendship like a weird dream.

'Hang on a minute!' shouted the Gypsy King as he disappeared from view. 'The thing I'm most afraid of in the world isn't THE POWER OF FRIENDSHIP AND HELPING EACH OTHER! The thing I'm most afraid of in the world is bees! How is this even happening, this doesn't make any sense at all! How is this working?'

But it was too late. And the very last Princess Snowflake saw of the Gypsy King was his proud boots as they disappeared beneath the flames. And then even the flames were gone and all that remained was the vast army of witches and the little black rock. And standing on the rock was –

'Gooseberry!' cried Princess Snowflake. 'Oh, and my parents as well, even though I've never seen you before, I recognise you!'

'Hello,' said Princess Snowflake's parents, 'we were snatched up by the Gypsy King on the day you were born and we have spent the last eleven years in his power.'

'How come I didn't see you in little glass beads dangling from the chain around his neck?' said Princess Snowflake. 'Like Gooseberry was?'

'He turned us into, like, sort of, these kind of little red stones, well, not exactly stones, but kind of *like* stones, which he kept in his shirt pocket,' said Princess Snowflake's father. 'I don't know why, he must have one system for turning dogs into things and another system for dealing with people. Anyway, it's probably not that important, or not something we need to spend time worrying about right now. We're back at last!'

'Thank you for looking after our daughter

while we were away,' said Princess Snowflake's mother to the witches. 'I hope she wasn't any trouble.'

'She had her moments,' said Cobwep. But she said it with a smile.

'How lucky I am to have witches and parents and the prettiest little dog in the world!' cried Princess Snowflake. 'But best of all, I have learnt about friendship and accepting help from people.'

And Gooseberry barked three times: once for happiness to see his mistress again, once for joy to feel her arms around him again and once because it was a fairy tale and as you know, things always happen in threes in fairy tales. On Gooseberry's third bark, the Realm of the Gypsy King was gone and there they all were, back in the gardens of the Winter Palace, with the snow falling all around and the birds singing and Chomley the hedgehog snuffling for treats like always.

A deer bounded by with a big 'D' painted on its side. Then another one with 'A'. Then another, with 'N'. Then another, with 'G'. Then another, with 'E'. And then one more, with 'R' painted on its side.

'Oh, how wonderful,' laughed Princess Snowflake, clapping her hands together, one, two, three! 'It's those lovely deer again! Daniel and Arthur and Neil and Georgina and Eleanor and my favourite, Rum-Pum-Pum!'

And Princess Snowflake was right. That's exactly what those letters stood for. And when she grew up, Princess Snowflake married Rum-Pum-Pum, because it was the Age of Fairy Tales and you could do what you like back then, it was absolutely fine to marry a deer if you felt like it. Or a field, you could even marry a field if you fancied. And her parents moved back into the Winter Palace and Gooseberry became their butler, though he did charge quite a high price for his services.

In time, Princess Snowflake grew tired of the gardens and she rode Rum-Pum-Pum far and wide and together they had many more adventures and defeated all sorts of horrors, including the Flipsy King (who was a sort of evil pancake-making guy), the Chipsy King (who was like this nasty dude who owned a kebab shop but the portions were really small and he used to charge way too much for sachets of ketchup) and the Pipsy King (who was a sort of cross between a man and an apple and when you went near him he'd spit apple pips at you and if one hit you you would turn into an apple yourself but Princess Snowflake and Rum-Pum-Pum defeated him by saying, 'Hey, look over there, there's something really interesting!' and when the Pipsy King looked over there they quickly rushed up to him and Rum-Pum-Pum kicked him to death with his hooves). And Princess Snowflake and Rum-Pum-Pum had lots of children together, some were humans and some were deers, and some were humans but with just the legs of a deer, and one of them was a Smurf.

And they all lived happily ever after.

THE END

The Story of Old King Thunderbelly and the Wall of Lamonic Bibber

 ow, all this happened way back in the Dark Ages, when people still thought that the world was flat, not like today when we know it's a sort of giant shiny cube.

In those distant, ignorant times, the whole of England was ruled over by Old King Thunderbelly, who lived in a grand castle in the middle of Lamonic Bibber.

One day, Old King Thunderbelly was strolling in the castle courtyards, which were not as magnificent as you might think. They were just all right. The best bit was a Swingball, but even that wasn't brilliant because it kept tipping over if you whacked the ball too hard.

'I am so crafty,' said Old King Thunderbelly as he strolled around the courtyards. 'For a start, I'm the king of the whole of England. And for another start, I can outwit anyone who crosses my path.'

But at that moment a crow crossed Old King Thunderbelly's path.

'Oho,' said the crow. 'So you think you can outwit anyone, is that what I heard you say, you arrogant king?'

'Yes,' said Old King Thunderbelly. 'Why, have you got a challenge for me?'

'I certainly have,' remarked the crow. 'I bet you can't keep me out of Lamonic Bibber.'

'I bet I can,' said Old King Thunderbelly.

'I bet you can't,' said the crow.

'I bet I can,' said Old King Thunderbelly.

'No, seriously, I bet you can't,' said the crow.

'I really actually think I

can,' said Old King Thunderbelly.

'I bet you can't,' said the crow.

'I bet I can,' said Old King Thunderbelly.

'Listen,' said the crow, 'I honestly bet you can't.'

'No, you listen, you idiot,' said Old King Thunderbelly. 'I bet I can.'

'I bet you can't,' said the crow.

'I bet I can,' said Old King Thunderbelly.

Well, this argument went on for a day and a night and it was the most boring day and night either of them had ever spent, until eventually the crow said, 'OK, then, king-features. Prove it. I will walk ten miles out of town and then I will try to get back in.

And just you see if you can stop me.'

'All right, I will,' said Old King Thunderbelly.

So the crow turned around and started walking out of town. And Old King Thunderbelly began to make his plans.

᷿ ❁ ᷿

'I will build a mighty wall all around Lamonic Bibber,' said Old King Thunderbelly to himself. 'How can a crow possibly get over a wall? It's impossible. And I will put some guards at the entrances and I will give them strict orders not to let in any crows. My God, I'm crafty!' he said, rubbing his hands together, which was the first time a crafty person had ever rubbed his hands together to show he was doing crafty things.

'Now, how will I build a wall?' mused Old King Thunderbelly. 'I know! I'll get my friend

John to do it for me.'

Now this was certainly a wonderful idea, because Old King Thunderbelly's friend John was a famous wall-builder, known far and wide for his enormous farts. And also for how good he was at building walls.

So Old King Thunderbelly took out some bits of wood and a hammer and a few bells and he invented the world's first telephone. Then he invented the world's second telephone. Then he went round to his friend John's house and gave John a telephone.

'What's this?' said John.

'You'll see,' winked Old King Thunderbelly. Then he went back to his palace and dialled John's number.

'Hello,' said Old King Thunderbelly. 'Is that John?'

'No, it's his wife,' said the voice at the other end of the line. 'I'll just go and get John, he's having a fart in the shed.'

'OK,' said Old King Thunderbelly.

Soon John came to the phone.

'Hello,' said John.

'Hello,' said Old King Thunderbelly. 'Do you like this new invention? It's called a "telephone".'

'Yeah, it's brilliant,' said John. 'Now, what can I do for you today, Your Highness? Do you want me to build a wall or something?'

'Yes,' said Old King Thunderbelly. 'I want you to build a wall around Lamonic Bibber.'

'Why, have you accepted a challenge from a crow or something?' said John.

'John, you know me well,' laughed Old King Thunderbelly. 'I certainly have.'

About three weeks later the wall was finally

finished. John had worked day and night to build it, and it was probably the best wall he'd ever built. It was made out of stone and it was really high and there were spikes on it and every few hundred yards there were signs saying 'NO CROWS ALLOWED' and 'KEEP OUT IF YOU ARE A CROW'. There were two gates set into the wall and at each gate stood two beefy guards, each holding a sharp silver sword, except for one of them who had forgotten his sword and was holding a massive garlic bread covered in tinfoil instead and hoping nobody would notice.

'Now let's see that crow try and get in,' laughed Old King Thunderbelly.

❧ ❀ ☙

Presently a traveller came up to the South Gate of the Wall of Lamonic Bibber. He was dressed in a fine coat of feathers and he had a beak and two wings and he was about the size of a crow.

'Hello,' said the traveller to the guards. 'Do you mind if I come in through your gate?'

'No, go ahead, we don't care,' said the guards. 'Go right in.'

But as the traveller stepped forward, the first guard thought of something.

'Hang on a minute,' he said. 'You're not a crow, are you?'

'Who, me?'

laughed the traveller. 'No, of course not.'

'OK, sorry to bother you,' said the first guard. But just as the traveller was about to step inside, the second guard thought of something.

'Hang on,' he said, brandishing his sword. 'You *are* a crow. Go away! It's no crows allowed, those are our orders!'

'Blast those guards,' sulked the crow as he walked off. 'They're cleverer than they look. How am I going to get into Lamonic Bibber now?'

Well, that crow thought for a year and a day, and it was the most boring year and a day he'd ever spent. But eventually he came up with an absolutely brilliant idea, and when he came up with it a light bulb appeared above his head, and that's

how electricity was invented.

'I've got it!' said the crow.

⋰ ❈ ⋱

About five years later, Old King Thunderbelly was sitting in the castle courtyards, having a sandwich and congratulating himself on outwitting the crow.

'That was totally easy,' he said to himself. 'That wall did the trick no problem. It's been years and years now and I still haven't seen that crow around here.'

'Oh, haven't you?' said a voice at that very moment. And looking down, Old King Thunderbelly was astonished to see none other than the crow himself, the very crow he'd been trying to keep out all this time!

'How did you get in here?' said Old King

Thunderbelly. 'Surely my wall should have kept you out?'

'Well might you think so, king,' said the crow. 'But there's one thing you forgot about us crows,' he continued, flapping his powerful wings triumphantly. 'We are excellent at digging. I have spent the past five years digging a tunnel under that wall with my beak and finally I have won the challenge and you must give me all the land of the kingdom and let me marry your daughter and you must be my slave forever and fetch me rare minerals.'

'I don't remember saying anything about that,' said Old King Thunderbelly. 'But OK.'

And that is how the elephant got its trunk.

THE END

700 AD

Life and ++ Times Of ++ Saint Follican+

(As written by Bene The Elder,
a stinking old monk of the
Order Of The Prawn)

ello. It is me, Bene The Elder, a very un-smelly monk (despite what thou mayeth hath heard) of the Order Of The Prawn, which is the finest of all the orders of monks in the whole of Lamonic Bibber and we hath gotteth the best robes and sandals, much better than all the other monks, who boughteth cheap ones from Matalan. Now readeth thee my amazing words that I am writing on parchment with my quill that is madeth of the finest goat feathers. For now shall I tell of one who was borneth in Lamonic Bibber and of those deeds and wonders that he did performeth and which were known as true Miracles Of The Lord.

For yea, the one of whom I speak wast to our people what the sun is even to the Heavens and, yea, what the rain is even to the crops and, yea, what the piece of cheese is even to the greedy man who cannot sleepeth and who quite fancieth a piece of cheese after midnight even though he knoweth it will giveth him horrible dreams about being hounded by a terrifying snail, as did happeneth to me only a few nights ago. And, yea, he wast just generally excellent. (Saint Follican, I meaneth, not the snail.)

🌿 Birth Of Saint Follican 🌿

Knoweth that this blessed one wast truly called Saint Follican and so it did come to pass that he wast born in a filthy donkey field in the middle of Lamonic Bibber some number of years before I write these words. Saint Follican's mother wast but a poor woman with a face like a chip shop and when her baby son did poppeth out she was heardeth to exclaim, 'Oh, look! I accidentally done a Saint, that's nice.'

❧ First Miracle Of Saint Follican ❧

Saint Follican wast born with a glorious halo encirclingeth his head which did gloweth brightly all day and all night long. But after a few weeks the batteries did runneth out and Saint Follican did throweth away his halo and it did go spinning far over the fields and it wast caughteth in the teeth of a cow who wast called Bosky.

And the people of Lamonic Bibber did rejoiceth and cry, 'It is a Miracle, Saint Follican hath inventedeth the Frisbee, even though he is but one month old.' And from that day on,

Saint Follican did becometh very famous and the peasants of the land did travel from near and far to see him, in hope that he might be able to cureth their ills.

❧ Second Miracle Of Saint Follican ❧

Even though Saint Follican never could cureth any of the peasants' ills (and sometimes he actually did maketh them slightly worse because he did haveth baby germs), everyone did agree that he wast a nice baby with a funny nose, so at least that did cheereth them up a bit. And so the Cheeringeth Up Of The Peasants A Bit did cometh to be known as the Second Miracle Of Saint Follican. (Some might not think that it was much of a Miracle, but truly it wast, for it is very difficult to getteth a peasant to smile even a little bit because they are always goingeth on and on and on about how they haven't gotteth any money or food, or how one of their arms hath just fallen off because they've gotteth leprosy or something. Generally they are an ungrateful lot, why don'teth they just eateth their own arms if they're so hungry, that's what I'd liketh to know? And they are ugly too, some of them looketh like unto potatoes.)

🌿 Third Miracle Of Saint Follican 🌿

One day when Saint Follican wast but three years old, it did so happeneth that an old man called the Wise Man Of Asterly did travel from the neighbouring village of Asterly for to visit him, and he did findeth the child sitting in the dirt doing a big poo. And when the Wise Man Of Asterly did spyeth this poo laying upon the ground, he did rejoiceth

and picketh it up and holdeth it high above his head for all to wonder at and he did cryeth, 'It is the THIRD MIRACLE OF SAINT FOLLICAN!'

But the peasants did rejoineth, 'No, it is just a poo, that does not count as a Miracle.'

And then the Wise Man Of Asterly did discerneth that he was not quite as wise as he had thoughteth and that he was just holding a big poo and he did immediately returneth home to his village and from that day forth he was knowneth not as the Wise Man Of Asterly but indeed he was christened 'Brownhand', and he did liveth out the last days of his life as a laughing-stock, for from that day forth every time someone in Asterly did doeth a poo, they would exclaimeth, 'Come quick, Brownhand, for I have done a "Miracle", maybe you would like to inspect it!' And thus did Brownhand dieth in shame and in loneliness and in a hedge.

But a few years later, when Saint Follican wast eight years of age, he wast granted a most wondrous strength, and thus did the Strength Of Twenty Men becometh the actual Third Miracle and many wast the peasant who wast much amazed to spyeth the child pulling up a tree by its roots and throwing it unto the Heavens, from whence never it cameth back down; or doingeth such a powerful karate chop on a horse that the animal did shattereth into a thousand tiny horses.

(But exactly one year later Saint Follican's strength did returneth to normal, so the Third Miracle Of Saint Follican did turneth out to be a bit of a letdown. It wast still a Miracle, but it wasn't one of those Miracles that lasteth forever, it dideth have an expiry date.)

❧ Fourth Miracle Of Saint Follican ❧

As Saint Follican did groweth older, so he did groweth taller, but that wast not a Miracle, that is just what happeneth when a child groweth from a boy into a man. (Or what happeneth when a girl groweth into whatever it is that girls groweth up to become, maybe a large piece of metal or something? I hath no idea about girls and things because I am a monk.)

And also as he did groweth older, Saint Follican did groweth a beard upon his face and that wast not a Miracle either, that is also just what happeneth when people groweth up. It is natural and good, for well it is written in the

Holy Bible: *As the child doth groweth from boy to man, so he doth getteth stubble on his chin and his voice doth goeth funny and he doth sitteth in his room all day sulking and listeningeth to depressing music; and many are the spots on his face.*

But also as he did groweth older, Saint Follican did groweth a beard upon someone *else's* face, and thus the Beard That Did Belongeth To Saint Follican But Which Did Groweth On Another Man's Face did cometh to be known as the Fourth Miracle.

❧ Fifth Miracle Of Saint Follican ❧

One day Saint Follican did starteth being able to talketh to sheep, and thus the Understanding Of What Sheep Are Saying When They Goeth 'Baaa! Baaaaa! Baaaaaaa!

Baaaaaa! Baaaaaaaaa! Baaa! Baaaaa! Baaaaaa! Baaaaaaaaaaaaaaaaaaaaa!' did cometh to be known as the Fifth Miracle.

(And furthermore, it was at this time too that Saint Follican did for some time avoideth the company of people and instead hangeth about with three lowly sheep of the highlands, who were his only friends. And these sheep he did nameth Anthony, Stephen and Matthew. And one day Matthew did giveth birth to a tiny lamb and then Saint Follican did decideth to rename Matthew, 'Harriet'. But of what else Saint Follican did getteth up to at this time in his life, only the sheep doth know.)

~~Sixth Miracle Of Saint Follican~~

~~One day Saint Follican did starteth being able to walk on water, except he usually~~

~~felleth in and becameth wet like unto a normal~~
~~person, so — maybe a Miracle? Or maybe not?~~
~~There is some debate. Probably not, actually.~~
~~Forgeteth that one.~~

Sorry about that, hangeth on, let me just goeth back and crosseth that last one out, right, here's some more Miracles Of Saint Follican, proper ones this time

One day Saint Follican did haveth a long chat with God on top of a mountain, which wast most definitely a Miracle, one of the biggest Miracles of all time, so big that it did counteth for three Miracles. And thus the Chat With God On Top Of A Mountain did becometh known as the Sixth, Seventh and Eighth Miracles.

To this day no one (not even the sheep) doth know what God and Saint Follican did chatteth about. But truly it is reckoned that they did enjoyeth some snacks whilst they did talketh, because this monk I knoweth called Thomas The Liar did telleth me that he wast walking on the mountainside later that same afternoon and he did findeth a Holy Empty Packet Of Jaffa Cakes and some Holy Used Tea Bags that they had lefteth behind.

✖ Ninth Miracle Of Saint Follican ✖

One day when Saint Follican wast a man of some thirty years of age, he wast invited to a great wedding at the town of Wample-Upon-Stample, some miles to the west of Lamonic Bibber. It wast to be a great feast, with many hundreds of guests, but when he did arriveth, he did findeth all the multitudes up in arms and the groom crying, 'What is to becometh of us, for I hath forgotten to ordereth enough to feed so many guests.' And the groom did showeth Saint Follican what he had orderedeth, which wast merely one pizza made by the monks of the Holy Order Of Saint Domino, it wast of a large size and it did haveth a 'stuffed crust', but it wast still not enough to feedeth five thousand people.

Then did Saint Follican taketh the pizza from the hands of the groom and proclaimeth, 'I am just going to sit behind this rock for awhile.' And about half an hour later he did emergeth from behind the rock with quite a lot of sauce around his mouth and a bit of pepperoni in his beard and he did sayeth, 'I hath done another Miracle. I hath eaten the whole pizza by myself to teacheth you a valuable lesson that marriage is not about feasts. It is about the love we feeleth for each other in our hearts.'

And hearing this, the wedding guests did weepeth with gratitude and hunger that Saint Follican had saved them from greed and temptation. And they did rejoiceth and danceth and celebrateth the love they felt for one another in their hearts (except a few of them, including the groom, did droppeth dead of starvation). So the true Miracle wast not that Saint Follican did eateth an entire pizza, it was that he did manageth to get away with it without anyone punching him in the face, it is what is knowneth in the trade as a bit of a 'Cheeky Miracle'.

❧ Tenth And Final Miracle Of Saint Follican ❧

Knoweth thee that Saint Follican did not performeth many more Miracles after the wedding at Wample-Upon-Stample, for he did not want to pusheth his luck. But when he wast an old man of eighty years or more, he did announceth that he wast going to giveth one last performance, and knoweth thee that many tens of thousands of peasants came from all over these British Isles to witness this miraculous feat. But when they gotteth there and paideth their money, even though they didn't even haveth any money, it wast just Saint Follican in a top hat with a little puppet called 'Naughty Roger' sittingeth on his knee and Saint Follican wast pretendingeth that Naughty Roger wast saying things, like Saint Follican would goeth, 'Sayeth "hello" to the nice peasant boys and girls, Roger,' and Roger would goeth, 'Gnallo, boysangnurls,' only everyone could discerneth Saint Follican's lips moving and soon did they commenceth to boo and throweth pigs and dirt at him and thus Saint Follican did endeth his professional career runningeth away over the fields with a crowd of angry peasants chasing him with sticks.

❧ Death Of Saint Follican ❧

Saint Follican did runneth from the peasants all the way to the high cliffs which lieth to the east of Lamonic Bibber and there he did trippeth over his own beard and falleth into the sea, where he wast instantly consumedeth by prawns. And so it is that the prawn is regardedeth as the most Holy of all creatures that do walketh or flieth or swimmeth or bounceth on God's great Earth. And thus was the Order Of The Prawn establishedeth to honour the name of Saint Follican for now and for ever more and I am proud to counteth myself amongst that number. For, yea, Saint Follican wast truly the most glorious of all the Saints, much better than any of the other ones, for instance Saint George, whom everyone doth say did slayeth a fire-breathing Dragon. But I hath heard (from Thomas The Liar) that it was only an earthworm smoking a cigar, so shutteth up if you thinketh Saint George wast so great, he wast useless, why don't you marryeth Saint George if you loveth him so much.

Here Endeth the History
Of Saint Follican

Bibbering Through The Ages
Ráðghöldeskvúldrr

Ráðghöldeskvúldrr, or 'Ráðghöldeskvúldr' for short, was the chief of the Viking army that invaded Lamonic Bibber at the end of the eighth century. In battle she carried a huge broadsword in each hand; a broadsword clasped between the toes of each foot; a few more broadswords in her pocket in case the other ones got stuck in someone's forehead; an emergency broadsword

Artist's impression of a typical day in Ráðghöldeskvúldrr's life

hidden in her hair; and another emergency broadsword hidden inside the first emergency broadsword. According to writings unearthed at her burial mound, her nickname was 'Broadsword', although no one today knows why. Ráðghöldeskvúldrr was probably the most violent Viking warrior who ever lived, but there was far more to her than simply being extremely skilful at killing people in battle – she was also extremely skilful at killing people when she wasn't in battle. It is estimated that in her lifetime, Ráðghöldeskvúldrr slaughtered over ten thousand men, women and horses. In Old Norse, the language spoken by the Vikings, her name means 'The Lady of Peace'.

A BRIEF HISTORY
❧ *of the* ❧
MERRIE
OLD KINGS
❧ *and* ❧
QUEENS *of*
ENGLAND

For as long as anyone can remember, England has been absolutely stuffed full of kings and queens. In fact, England is probably one of the kingandqueeniest countries of all time and that's definitely a proper word.

The first ever King of England was a four-year-old boy known as **John of the Playground**, who liked to stand on slightly higher bits of ground than other people and say, 'Ha ha, I'm taller than you.' One day in the middle of the fourth century, he added, 'Oh, and by the way, I'm the King of England too.' No one had ever heard of kings before but they believed him anyway and so it was that John of the Playground ruled over England until suppertime, when he forgot all about being king because it was fish fingers that night and he was starving.

The second King of England was **King Sizebed**, who died after a few thousand people in Cornwall got a bit confused and all piled on top of him one evening. After him came **King Arthur**, who might not actually have been a real person, no one knows. After King Arthur came

King Pomegranates, who certainly wasn't a real person, he was just a bunch of pomegranates wearing a robe. And after him was **Old King Thunderbelly**, whom you may have read about elsewhere.

The next important one that anyone really remembers is **King Harold**, who turned up in 1066 and said, 'Hello. I should be the next king because look, my name's already King Harold,' and everyone agreed except one guy called **William the Conqueror** who travelled over from France on a picture of a ship drawn on a tapestry and said, 'Oh, so you're the king, are you? Well, I should probably conquer you now because look, my name's already William the Conqueror,' and with that he killed King Harold by shooting him in the thigh with a sparrow. William the Conqueror ruled England for about twenty years before eventually dying of not being alive any more.

After him, everyone decided they'd had enough of kings for the time being and maybe it was time to try a few queens out, sort of like when you get a bit sick of Salt & Vinegar, and move over to Cheese & Onion for a bit. And for the next hundred years or so, it was queen after queen after queen: **Queen Jane**, **Queen Mary**, **Queen Samantha**, **Queen Tina**, **Queen Caroline**, **Queen's Greatest Hits**, **Queen Matilda**, **Queen Miss Honey**, **Queen The BFG**, **Queen George's Marvellous Medicine**, and then Queen Jane again but a different one this time called **Queen Jane II: The Revenge**. In 1185 Queen Jane II: The Revenge fell in love with a handsome German royalty guy called **Prince Johan** and gave birth to a fat little baby who was known as

The Hamburger Heir and stunk of planks.

Meanwhile, Queen Jane II: The Revenge's cousin, a low-born knave by the name of **Tony Dustbins**, was plotting to strangle everyone in the court, so Prince Johan went and hid in a bush to escape, and there he began laying his own plans to become king. Then this guy called Paddles McKenzie sneaked up on Tony Dustbins from behind and licked him to death and then Paddles McKenzie killed Queen Jane II: The Revenge with a poisoned gun and he became **King Paddles McKenzie** and locked himself in a tower for nine months and gave birth to **King Henry VIII** and then King Henry VIII married himself six times and chopped his own head off twice and meanwhile another king broke into the kitchens and ate all the salt, which made him burst into flame and to this day no one knows his name or what on earth he even thought he was up to, and all the while, Prince Johan was still hiding in a bush, biding his time and laying his plans to become king.

Then another king got trapped by **a queen who was really a witch** and then the Crown Jewels were eaten by a swan and when the swan was cut open all the jewels had turned into princesses, and they grew up and were known as the **Seven Weird Magic Swan Princess Jewel Things of England** and they ruled until 1348 before disappearing into a hole in the sky, and then King Harold came back to life and built a castle out of his own hair and a princess climbed up King Harold's hair and when she got to the top, King Harold killed her and put on her dress and became **Queen King Harold**, and William the Conqueror tried to come back to life to conquer her/him again but he couldn't manage it because not everyone can.

Then another guy called Uncle Egg stabbed Queen King Harold in the heart with a bomb and then in 1412 **King Uncle Egg** went to a banquet where he didn't know anyone and died of embarrassment, and all the while, Prince Johan was still hiding in a bush, biding his time and laying his plans to become king.

Then a new king called **The Flash Panache** flew down on a rope and pounded everyone to death with a crossbow except for a baby called **Princess Nappies** who managed to escape to France where she learnt how to make baguettes and then she came back on a boat and gave the Flash Panache one of the baguettes, and when he tasted it he fell in love with it and married the baguette and for the next ninety years England was ruled by **a partially eaten baguette**, and then in 1636 a fellow called **King Stephen the Paranoid** took over and he was so paranoid about someone killing him to become king that he spent all his time plotting to kill himself so that he could become king even though he was already king, and one day he sneaked up on himself while he wasn't looking and killed himself, and for the next few years England was ruled by **King the Ghost of King Stephen the Paranoid** until in 1697 he killed himself so that he could become king, and for the next hundred and forty years England was ruled by **King the Ghost of the Ghost of King Stephen the Paranoid**, and all the while, Prince Johan was still hiding in a bush, biding his time and laying his plans to become king and then in 1837 **Queen Victoria** appeared out of nowhere in a hot-air balloon and took over the world until 1901 when she died after eating an infected leg and then **King Edward XIVVIXXCCVDDDDDDDDDDDDDDDD DDDDXXXXXXXXIIIIIIIIIIIII** became king, only he didn't really enjoy it because he had to sign his name on so many documents that his hand got tired and fell off and then **Queen Elizabeth II** jumped on the throne during a game of musical chairs and sat there for absolutely ages and then, in 2012, just when no one was expecting it, Prince Johan came out from the bush where he'd been hiding for hundreds and hundreds of years, biding his time and laying his plans to become king, and fell over and died of a sprained nose.

THE END

The Two Friends

O nce there were two friends, and nothing could come between them. They were equally handsome, equally tall, equally good at getting a bit of apple which had got stuck between their teeth out again by biting off a bit of their fingernail and just sort of wiggling it around in there until the bit of apple came out, equally good at saying to each other, 'Guess what? I just got a bit of apple out from between my teeth by biting off a bit of my fingernail and just sort of wiggling it around in there until the bit of apple came out', equally rich and equally full of fun and merriment. And they had been born on the very same day and they had known each other all their lives and they were even more fond of each other than they were of themselves.

Now, these two fine fellows' names were Orlando de Poisson and Arthuro del Arthuro del Arthuro del Arthuro del Arthuro del Arthuro del Arthuro. And one day they found themselves walking through the Forest of Runtus, on the outskirts of Lamonic Bibber. It was the Medieval Times, and everywhere you looked there were jesters. Millions of jesters, all over the place. And there were loads of knights having tournaments to see who was the best at dying by being killed in a tournament. And there were castles on every hillside and brightly coloured banners flying from every turret. Oh, and dragons. There were absolutely tons of dragons. It was brilliant. And if you killed a dragon you got five thousand points.

So anyway. There were Orlando and Arthuro, walking through the Forest of Runtus, proud as you please in their fancy clothes, both wearing big floppy hats, one with a red feather in the hatband, and one with a gold feather in the hatband and one with a blue feather in the hatband because Arthuro was actually wearing two big floppy hats.

'All is well with the world, Arthuro,' said Orlando happily, chewing on a jester as they walked. 'And even if it's not – even if there are wars and people without enough food and things – I don't give a fig! I just like to sing and dance and gad about all the livelong day.'

'Me too,' laughed Arthuro, quickly jumping on a horse and having a tournament with about twenty knights and killing them all in one go. 'The real world is not for me. I just like to cavort and caper with you, my dear Orlando, for you are like a brother to me.'

The two friends had now come to an archway formed by two low branches, all covered in roses. Stepping through, they found themselves in a clearing full of pleasant forest things, like a babbling brook and some flowers and a couple of magpies playing lutes. In the middle of the clearing stood a mighty cherry tree, and next to it an ancient stone statue of a goat, which leant crookedly in the long grass.

'What is this place?' said Arthuro. 'Is it a magic place that makes you say everything twice? What is this place? Is it a magic place that makes you say everything twice?'

'No,' said Orlando, killing a dragon as he spoke and getting five thousand points, which he immediately spent on sweetmeats. 'You're just being silly. But I feel that this is a place of great power, and it makes me think about important things like friendship and long grass. Come,' said he, growing suddenly serious. 'Let us make a solemn vow that nothing will ever come between us. Not wars, nor floods, nor a cake.'

'Why would a cake come between us?' frowned Arthuro.

'I've no idea, but let's put it in the vow just to be on the safe side,' said Orlando. 'Good

Arthuro, do you swear that nothing will ever come between us?'

'I swear it,' said Arthuro solemnly. 'Good Orlando, we shall remain friends forever, you and I.'

'Mere words mean nothing, you impossible donkey!' said Orlando, and he snatched up two acorns from the forest floor and handed one to Arthuro. 'Let us swear our friendship for each other by these acorns. Now say it along with me.'

And so the two friends stood there, illuminated by a shaft of sunlight which fell between the leaves of the trees in that magical clearing, and they clutched their acorns tightly to their foreheads as they made their vow:

I do swear, by the acorns that grow 'pon
the ground in this lovely place, that nothing

shall ever come between us. Not wars, nor floods, nor a cake. We shall always be friends, united together, come what may.

5000 pts

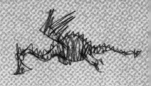

No sooner had they spoken these words
than the most beautiful lady either of them
had ever seen emerged from behind a weeping
willow, where she had been washing her long
chestnut hair. She was barefoot, and clad in
a gown as light as gossamer, and she wore no

jewellery anywhere about her person, for neither silver nor gold could possibly have added to her beauty. The solemnness of the vow was forgotten – in an instant both men were hopelessly in love.

'Hello, Orlando and Arthuro,' said the maiden. 'My name is Ursula La Treymin. Long have I waited for a fine young man to arrive in this place and marry me and make my heart sing and stroke my hair and kiss my elbows and feed me jesters all day long. But what am I to do, because there are two of you and only one of me, so it won't really work so forget it, I think I'll just go off and be eaten by a dragon instead.'

'No, pray you stay!' shouted Orlando and Arthuro together, and they fell to their knees and threw their arms out like wild crisps.

'Marry me, sweet lady,' said Orlando, 'for I love thee like the stars.'

'No, my lady, marry me,' said Arthuro, 'for I love thee like the moon.'

'I love thee like the sun,' said Orlando.

'Me too,' said Arthuro,' I love thee like the stars AND the moon AND the sun, all blended up together into one gigantic "space milkshake". Plus, I've got two hats, far better than someone like Orlando, for example, who's only got one hat.'

'Hee hee hee,' laughed the lady Ursula, throwing back her silky chestnut hair. 'You two are silly ninnies! I cannot marry the both of you. But how shall I decide between such equally matched suitors? Aha! I have it!'

For just one moment the sky clouded over, and the lady's face seemed suddenly to turn strange, as if it were just as goatish and wild as the statue which stood in that place – but then the illusion passed.

'You must fight in a duel to the death,' said the lady Ursula. 'A year and a day from now, you must return to this clearing and you must be sitting on amazing horses and you must be covered in shining armour and have sharp lances in your hands and hatred on your faces and you must attack each other and whichever one of you wins the day shall win me too. Now – get thee gone from this place!' cried she. 'I shall see you next at the battle.'

So Orlando and Arthuro turned away from each other and off they went to practise their fighting. And over the following weeks and months, each of them grew so strong and so bold that the villagers of Lamonic Bibber marvelled to see it.

'Look at Orlando and Arthuro,' said the friar, Jonathan De Rypls, the fattest and most religious man in town. 'Their muscles have grown so large that they are like cartwheels!'

'I think their muscles are so large that they are as big as elephants, in far-off lands,' said a little girl called Medieval Peter.

'Just look at their muscles,' said Martyn Woodenmangle, who owned a wooden mangle

which he used for washing people's clothes. 'They are so large that they are like cartwheels!'

'Oi,' said Jonathan De Rypls, 'stop stealing my ideas, Martyn.'

'Are you going to sit on me to teach me a lesson?' trembled Martyn Woodenmangle.

'No,' said Jonathan De Rypls religiously. 'It is not my place to sit on you, Martyn. But God will sit on you when you die. And he's massive.'

A full year had now passed since Orlando and Arthuro had encountered the lovely maiden. There was but one more day before they returned to do battle for her hand in marriage. But now, so close to the appointed time, neither man could rest, but instead went walking alone through the Forest of Runtus to steady their nerves.

'Just wait until tomorrow,' said Orlando as he walked through the forest, chopping down fully-grown trees just by looking at them with his muscles. 'I'm going to show that stupid Arthuro what's what, that's what!'

'That simpleton Orlando had better look out,' said Arthuro as he strode along, knocking down jesters just by holding up a sign saying 'I'VE GOT ENORMOUS MUSCLES'. 'Tomorrow his number's up! Tomorrow I'm going to –'

But at that moment their paths crossed and they regarded each other in horrified astonishment. For as each man stood there, gazing upon his foe, it was like looking into a terrible mirror and they realized what they had become.

'Oh, Arthuro, Arthuro!' sobbed Orlando. 'Can this be the kindly Arthuro that once I did know like a brother, who did love to play with daisies and who did once let a butterfly live in his ear for over ten years merely because it seemed to like it there?'

'And you, Orlando!' wept Arthuro. 'You, with your face all screwed up with hatred, and your muscles all screwed up with muscles! And yet once thou were so gentle that I did see thee sit on an abandoned goose egg for nearly a month until a gosling hatched, and then thou did become its mother and teach it to swim.'

'Look what we have done!' cried the two men. 'We have allowed something to come between us after all – a maiden!' They fell in to each other's arms and wept all their hatred away, and as they did so, the sun came out and a wonderful music seemed to fill the entire forest. And looking down, they saw a young boy, dressed as a jester but in every colour of the rainbow.

'Young men,' said the boy, though he was far younger than either of them. 'At last you have seen the truth. You are much too good to fight and kill each other, for that is the way of ignorance and fear. Tomorrow when you face one another in combat, you must embrace a nobler way and tell Ursula La Treymin that you will not fight after all. And now I must leave you, for my Uncle Francis is having a barbeque at his castle. Fare thee well, brave Orlando and Arthuro, fare thee well!'

Off he ran, and where he had stood lay two fruits upon the ground – a tiny apple and a tiny pear, each one glazed with delicious caramel and sesame seeds. And the two friends ate those candied fruits and chewed on them well and they fell asleep in the forest, and slept like babes in each other's arms. And when the next day dawned they walked hand in hand through the rose-covered archway and there, together in the forest clearing, they faced Ursula La Treymin once more.

'Well?' she demanded. 'Are you ready to fight to the death for the honour of marrying me?'

'Fair lady, we are not,' proclaimed Orlando. 'For we have realised that we are the best of friends after all, and nothing may ever come between us – not wars, nor floods, nor a cake.'

'Nor even a beautiful lady such as yourself,' finished Arthuro with a bow.

'Then you have passed my test,' said Ursula La Treymin. 'Because look at the letters in my name. If you rearrange them it spells out "I AM REALLY RUNTUS".'

And with that, Ursula La Treymin sort of dissolved, kind of like that bit in *Raiders of the Lost Ark* when all the baddies' faces start melting. And in her place stood a curious figure with a quick, mischievous smile, and curly hair and the shaggy legs of a goat.

'Runtus, the ancient woodland spirit who rules over the wild groves and forests!' gasped Orlando and Arthuro as one.

'Yes,' laughed Runtus, bringing a flute to his lips and playing three quick notes in delight. 'It was all just a game to see if I could turn two friends against each other.'

'And you have passed *my* test!' laughed

Orlando and he sort of dissolved too, and in his place stood a magnificent dragon, three hundred feet long and all covered in scales of gold and with eyes of pure diamonds. 'For I am the mighty Dominicus, the king of all the dragons in the world! I have been pretending to be Orlando for these last thirty years, just to see if I could trick Arthuro into believing I was a man!'

And then an acorn that was lying in the grass turned into a man and said, 'Ha ha ha! And you have passed *my* test, Dominicus! Because I am the real Orlando! I have been pretending to be an acorn,

I can't even remember why, but anyway, here I am now!'

And then the sun turned into the moon and said, 'Ha ha ha! You have all passed *my* test! Because it is not daytime at all, it's the middle of the night! I have been pretending to be the sun, I can't really remember why either, but I just have!'

And then about a hundred jesters all turned into centaurs and the trees in the clearing turned into unicorns and then Runtus turned into a library by accident and then turned back into Runtus, except he still had a couple of books stuck to his face and a shelf growing out of his knee.

And Arthuro, who was not pretending to be anything at all, stood there scratching his head in wonder at the whole thing.

'I hate the Medieval Times,' he said. 'You can't trust anyone.'

The End

Bibbering Through The Ages
UPSIDE-DOWN WALKER ON THE BUN SHOP

Upside-Down Walker on the Bun Shop was the world's first ever superhero. He lived on top of the bun shop in Lamonic Bibber from 1309 to 1353 and his best friend was a pebble who secretly hated him. Because he was the world's first superhero, Upside-Down Walker on the Bun Shop's superpowers weren't very good. He could never leave the bun shop roof; nor could he walk the right way up. All he could do was walk upside-down on the bun shop. He was good for nothing and when he died everyone was glad to see him go. Today his memory is kept alive by the Upside-Down Walker on the Bun Shop Appreciation Society, of which there are absolutely no members at all.

THE DUCKLING
and
HIS MOTHER

(FOURTEENTH-CENTURY POEM,
DISCOVERED IN A PLASTIC BAG
BURIED BY THE STONE TABLE)

'What is the best season?' asked the
    duckling of his mother,
' 'Tis summer, 'tis summer,'
    quacked she.
'For in the summer, it is nice and warm,
'And the river runs fast and free.

'And the swifts and the swallows fly high
   and wild,
'And they sing,' said his mother,
   'as they fly.
'And winter is gone,
   like a rubbish bad dream,
'And the days are hot and dry.'

'You are right,' quacked the duckling,
   ' 'tis summer that's best,
'It is truly the season of joy.
'I'm glad you're my mother,'
   he laughed in glee,
'Here's a picture I drew for you.
   I'm sorry it's not very good but
   I haven't got any hands.'

'TIS RUBBISH BEING A SQUIRREL

A Comedie written by William
Shakespeare's slightly less
well-known brother, Terry

DRAMATIS PERSONAE

The Duke of Lamonic Bibber.

MELISSA, *his daughter.*

PORKS, *a young man.*

A Hag.

A Squirrel.

A Shoe salesman.

VALENCIO, *a footservant.*

ACT I
SCENE I. ~ A Meadow. Enter PORKS.

PORKS

Oh, woe, woe. Now is the greatest
sadness I have ev'r known. For I am in
love with Melissa, who is the Duke's
daughter. But she is not in love with
me. Eh, what now is this? An old hag
approaches.

Enter a Hag.

HAG

Greetings, Porks.

PORKS

> How doth thou know'st mine name, hag?
> Art thou a magic hag?

HAG

> Yes. Tho' I am but a rough, smelly old hag
> who lives in a ditch, I am well-
> versed in the art of magic. Now,
> wouldst thou marry Melissa?

PORKS

> Truly I would. But she cares not for
> one such as I, for I am a low-born
> fellow and she dwells in great splendour
> at court.

HAG

> Well, thou must take this potion and
> slip it into her drink. 'T'will into a deep

slumb'r send her and when she doth
awake, she will fall in love with thee.

PORKS

How can I repay thee?

HAG

I demand nothing for my services but
that upon thy wedding day thou invite
me to the feast.

PORKS

What! Have an old hag at court? Hag,
thy face is like unto an old cheese
that is crawling with flies and worms.
Thou art far too ugly and hunch'd
up like a disgusting crab-apple
to appear in the company of great
dukes and nobles.

HAG

> Fine, I shall be on my way then,
> Porks. Good luck being lonely
> for the rest of your life, thou loser.

PORKS

> Pray, tarry! I did speak true – but
> perhaps I hath been hasty. Give the
> potion unto me.

HAG

> And thou willst to the
> wedding feast invite me?

PORKS

> I do swear it 'pon Melissa's life itself.

HAG

> OK, cool. Here you go. But be warn'd.
> If thou dost not this bargain keep, I shall

poison Melissa to death and thou will live
alone for the rest of thy days, knowing
that thou were the one who did
from this world take her.

PORKS

'Tis of no concern, hag, for I shall
ensure you def'nitely invited will be.

Exit PORKS.

HAG

And now we'll see how youthful
love is blind. For I hath set a trap,
Porks soon will find.

SCENE II. ~ The Royal Court.
MELISSA and her father the Duke
of Lamonic Bibber are at table.

MELISSA

Mmm, this is tasty food, Father.

DUKE

Yes, for we are rich and we can afford
the finest of everything, ha ha ha.

MELISSA

Guess who I'm never going to marry,
Father? 'Tis Porks. He is too poor. Ha
ha ha.

DUKE

Ha ha ha.

MELISSA

Ha.

*Enter PORKS, disguised as a marrow. He creeps
up on MELISSA and slips the Hag's potion into
her wine.*

MELISSA *(cont'd)*

> Mmm, this wine is so nice. I shall
> have another sip. Slurp. Slurp. Slu–
> Zzzz.

DUKE

> Why, she hath fallen asleep at table!

MELISSA

> Ah, what a nice nap.

DUKE

> Why, she hath awoken!

MELISSA

> Father, guess who I love? 'Tis Porks.
> I shall marry him.

DUKE

What! Only a moment ago you did say
how little you car'd for Porks.

MELISSA

Well, I like him now.

PORKS (*to himself*)

Ha! Most excellent hag! This potion
was a splendid idea. Now to sneak back
to the meadow.

Exit PORKS, disguised as a big box of plasters.

DUKE

This is exceeding strange. But very well,
the marriage feast shall be this Saturday.

SCENE III. ~ The Meadow.
PORKS sits alone.

PORKS

> She will be here any time now, I am
> sure – aha, here she comes.

Enter MELISSA.

MELISSA

> Oh, Porks, Porks! Thou art the fairest
> Porks! Thou art mine own dear Porks!
> How I do love thee, Porks.

PORKS (*to himself*)

> Methinks the plan was a success.

(*to Melissa*)

> Good day to you, Melissa. Shall we
> married be?

MELISSA

Yes, 'tis what I want most in the world.

PORKS

And I want it too, Melissa. I want it
more than I can tell thee with words
alone. What sayeth your father the
Duke of our joining?

MELISSA

He has declar'd that the wedding feast
shall be Saturday and that all in town
shall invit'd be.

PORKS

Ah, this is passing good!

MELISSA

Except for any hags. My father the
Duke does not like hags. He thinks

they are horrible, otherwise why would
they be called 'hags'? He has said
that if we invite any hags to the
feast, then no wedding shall there be.

PORKS

Oh, come off it. Really?

MELISSA

Yes, he was most clear on that one
point. ''Tis my only condition,' spake
he. ''Tis the only thing I ask. A
blessing on the union 'twixt you and
Porks,' spake he, 'but if thou dost
invite a hag to the wedding feast,
then 'tis all over and thou shall not
marry Porks and thou art no daughter
of mine and I shall banish thee
forever,' spake he.

PORKS

He doth go on a bit with all that
spaking, your dad, doth he not?

MELISSA

Yes, truly he is an irritating
chatterbox. But what of it, Porks,
my fondling? For we were not
planning to invite any hags to the
feast, surely!

PORKS

No, no, def'nitely not.

(to himself)

'Tis a disaster! For well it is
known that none can change the mind
of the Duke, he is the most stubborn
man in the kingdom. And now the hag
will not to the wedding invit'd be,

and she will to death Melissa poison.
But I must put a brave face on't and
work out a plan.

MELISSA

What are thou to thyself murmuring
about, sweet Porks?

PORKS

Oh, nothing.

MELISSA

OK, awesome. See you later, I have to
go back to court now and sit at
table. We are always sitting at table
at court, 'tis nice. And soon you will
be sitting at table with us, Porks, my
love.

Exit MELISSA.

PORKS

> What to do? For I see now that I
> hath by this foul hag been fool'd. I
> should never have into this
> bargain enter'd. I am trapp'd.

Enter a Squirrel.

SQUIRREL

> Hello, I am a squirrel. But why dost
> thou cry tears of water from thine
> eyes, Porks?

PORKS

> How dost thou know mine name,
> squirrel? Are thou a magic squirrel
> who can from mine predicament me
> help?

SQUIRREL

Yes, truly I am a magic squirrel, tho' I can do nothing about your appallingly confusing sentences. Yet I can a potion give thee, all thou hast to do is slip it into Melissa's father's drink and he will not mind if the hag to the feast comes.

PORKS

Hast everyone in this meadow got magic potions?

SQUIRREL

More or less, yes. It is called 'The Meadow Of Magic Potions', after all.

PORKS

Oh, right, I didn't know that, that makes total sense. Then I thank thee, kindly creature of nuts and bushy

tail. I shall take thy potion and to
the court hasten.

Exit PORKS.

SQUIRREL

So Porks unto the court with potion
goes. But soon he'll find I have but
doubl'd his woes.

SCENE IV. ~ The Court. MELISSA and the Duke are at table.

DUKE

Well, here we are at table again. Hath
thou told Porks about mine 'no hags' rule?

MELISSA

Yes, Father. He was fine with it,
methinks.

DUKE

> Then everything proceeds well. I
> shalt another sip of wine take.

*Enter PORKS, disguised as some toenails in a
fridge. He slips the potion into the Duke's wine
just as the Duke is about to take a sip.*

DUKE *(cont'd)*

> Slurp. Slurp. Slu– Zzzzz.

MELISSA

> What! Father! Thou hast fallen
> asleep at table!

DUKE *(waking)*

> Ah, now what was all that 'bout? Now,
> Melissa. Run and tell Porks that he must
> invite the hag to the wedding.

MELISSA

> What! Thou said only a moment
> before that he must not invite any hags.

DUKE

> Yes, but I hath chang'd my mind whilst
> I was a-snooze.

PORKS (*to himself*)

> Ha! This potion hath worked
> well. I am glad I did that squirrel trust.
> Now I can marry Melissa and the hag can
> come to the feast.

Exit PORKS, disguised as a drawing of a horse.

DUKE

> Oh, by the way, Melissa, when thou
> next see Porks, also tell him that instead
> of marrying you, he must now marry the
> squirrel.

MELISSA

But I am in love with Porks, Father!

DUKE

Yes, but I am your father, do what thou are told.

MELISSA

Oh, this is a horrid way to end Act I.

ACT II
SCENE I. ~ The Meadow.
PORKS is strolling, alone.

PORKS

> Alas and alack. I have now been
> trick'd by the hag and by the squirrel
> both. I have been trapp'd into
> marrying the squirrel, for Melissa did
> tell me that news and we both did weep
> when she spake it. This meadow is a
> curs'd place. That is the last magic potion
> I am accepting from anyone around here.

Enter a Shoe salesman.

SHOE SALESMAN

> Good morrow, Porks. I have here a
> magic potion that will help solve thy
> problem. Would you like it?

PORKS

> Yes, thank you, fine sir.

SHOE SALESMAN

> Thou hast only to slip it into the
> wine of both Melissa and her father
> the Duke as well.

PORKS

> Then I shall make haste!

Exit PORKS.

SHOE SALESMAN

This foolish lad does not learn from
mistakes. But ev'ry potion offer'd him
he takes.

SCENE II. ~ The Court. MELISSA and her father the Duke are at table.

MELISSA

Here we are again, at table.

DUKE

Yes, we are always at table.

MELISSA

I don't mind, 'tis a nice table to be at.

DUKE

I couldn't agree more.

MELISSA

But Father, I do ask again, may I not marry Porks?

DUKE

No! Porks must marry the squirrel, as I have said.

Enter PORKS, disguised as the Duke. He slips the potion into MELISSA's and the Duke's wine.

DUKE *(cont'd)*

Slurp, slurp, slu– Zzzz.

MELISSA

Slurp, slurp, slu– Zzzz.

PORKS

I shall 'scape before they wake.

Exit PORKS, disguised as Melissa. MELISSA and the Duke awake.

159

DUKE

> Strange that we should both fall
> asleep and then awak'n. We are always
> suddenly falling asleep at table and
> then suddenly waking up and changing
> our minds 'bout things.

MELISSA

> 'Tis true. I wonder if all of this falling
> asleep at table hath anything to do with
> the fact that we live right next door to
> the Meadow of Magic Potions.

DUKE

> Probably not. Now run and tell Porks
> that he can marry you after all and
> that thou can still invite the hag.

MELISSA

> Oh, Father, thank you! But I am weary of

all this going back and forth 'tween
meadow and court. I shall send my
footservant in my place. Valencio!

Enter VALENCIO.

VALENCIO

You called, mistress? What! Thou
seem'st a little bit smaller than usual.
And so do you, mine Duke.

DUKE

Smaller, sayest thou?

VALENCIO

I think so. 'Tis strange.

MELISSA

Never mind that now, Valencio. Run
and tell Porks the news.

ACT III
SCENE I. ~ *The edge of the Meadow.*
PORKS *is walking to the court.*

PORKS

> So! Valencio did tell me the good
> news. The wedding with Melissa is back
> on and the hag may come too. And now
> it is Saturday so off I go to the court.

Enter VALENCIO.

VALENCIO

> Porks! Porks! The wedding is off.

PORKS

What! But why?

VALENCIO

Well, you know Melissa and the Duke?

PORKS

No, I've never heard of them.

VALENCIO

What! Thou dost not know of whom I talk? The girl you are about to marry, like ten minutes from now? And her father?

PORKS

Oh, those guys. Sorry, yes, I did forget for a moment, Valencio.

VALENCIO

That's weird. Anyway, they have both

163

been shrinking since they were last at
table.

PORKS

What!

VALENCIO

Yes, truly, they are exceeding small
now, Porks. Look, I am holding them in
my hand.

PORKS

Why, they are the size of drawing
pins! This must the work of that last
potion be! I should never have trust'd that
shoe salesman. And that squirrel.
And that hag. Fie.

*Enter the Hag, with the Squirrel and the Shoe
salesman.*

HAG

Now hast thou seen the error of thy ways, Porks?

SQUIRREL

Thou art an idiot, Porks.

SHOE SALESMAN

We hath taught you a lesson about love, Porks. It cannot be won by magic potions, it has to be earn'd fair and square. Also, would you like to buy some shoes? Look at this fine pair I have here.

PORKS

No, I would not like to buy some sho–oh, those are quite nice actually. Hast thou got them in nine-and-a-halfs?

SHOE SALESMAN

Let me check, hang on.

Exit Shoe salesman.

PORKS

Now –

Re-enter Shoe salesman.

SHOE SALESMAN

I couldn't find any nine-and-a-halfs,
Porks. Care thee to try the nines?

PORKS

I think they will be a bit small, let
me – yes, they are a bit cramp'd at the
front, I have no room for my toes to
'breathe'. Now, back to the wedding
business. It seems to me –

SHOE SALESMAN

Care thee to try them in a ten?

PORKS

No, no, it was an idle fancy. Now,
back to the weddi–

VALENCIO

Go on, Porks, you may as well try
them. For they art nice shoes.

PORKS

'Tis true. Very well, I shall try the tens.

SQUIRREL

I don't suppose thou hast got any
size 'ones'?

SHOE SALESMAN

No, I don't have any squirrel-sized

shoes, sorry. But I shall fetch the
size tens for Porks.

Exit Shoe salesman.

SQUIRREL

'Tis a nightmare trying to find shoes
that will fit when thou art a squirrel.

PORKS

Oh, boo hoo hoo. Don't com'st thou
moaning to me, squirrel, thou were trying
to trick me into marrying thee.

SQUIRREL

'Tis true. Sorry about that.

Re-enter Shoe salesman.

SHOE SALESMAN

Here are the tens.

PORKS

> Let's see. Ah, not a bad fit at all!
> What dost thou think?

SHOE SALESMAN

> Very nice. Take a little walk about,
> see how they feel.

HAG

> Thou can use my magic mirror to see
> how they do look upon thy feet, Porks.

PORKS

> Thank you, hag. Yes, I shall take them.
> How much are they?

SHOE SALESMAN

> They are normally eight ducats, Porks.
> But because I trick'd you into
> shrinking Melissa and her father, I

shall for six let you them have.

PORKS

Thank you kindly, shoe salesman. I
hath no idea what a 'ducat' is but for
some reason mine pockets are full of
them. There you are.

SHOE SALESMAN

Shall I in the box for you them put?

PORKS

No, no, I shall wear them now. But canst
I the box have so that I may my
old shoes in them put?

SHOE SALESMAN

Yes, 'tis spoken wisely. Wouldst thou
like to purchase some leather-care
cream that will from scuffs the shoes

protect and in fine condition them
keep?

PORKS

No, thank you, I'm fine with just the
shoes.

HAG (*aside, to* Porks)

'Tis spoken wisely. The cream is a
total rip-off.

PORKS

Now, back to the wedding. Valencio,
even though thy mistress Melissa is
tiny I shall gladly marry her still. And even
though her father the Duke is tiny I
shall still take him as my father-in-law.

MELISSA

Hooray!

171

DUKE

Hooray!

HAG

Well done, Porks. Thou hast shown that thou know'st how to love, not with magic potions but because of from your heart. I shall Melissa and her father the right size make again. See how I do lightnings from my hands to zap them.

PORKS

That is so awesome. I did think that thou could only do stuff with magic potions.

HAG

No, I am well-vers'd in all sorts of magic.

PORKS

Can thou do lightnings from thy hands too, squirrel?

SQUIRREL

No, I can only do the magic potions.

PORKS

How about thee, shoe salesman?

SHOE SALESMAN

I cannot do lightnings from mine hands but I can 'pon occasion do enchant'd burps that make thieves become honest men if they do chance to smell them. Moreover, I can sometimes turn slightly invisible if I really conc'ntrate.

PORKS

So, everyone in the Meadow of Magic Potions can do the magic potions but the hag can do lots of other magic too and thou, shoe salesman, thou can do a few other tricks and the squirrel cannot

173

do anything except the magic potions?
Hath I got it straight?

SHOE SALESMAN

Yes.

PORKS

Isn't it wonderful how we are all
diff'rent.

MELISSA

Look, Father, we are back to normal size.

DUKE

'Tis truly said, Melissa.

MELISSA

And now to get married to Porks.

PORKS

Nae, I cannot do it.

MELISSA

What!

PORKS

I hath decided to marry the shoe salesman instead.

ALL EXCEPT PORKS

What!

MELISSA

But why, Porks?

PORKS

I don't know, Melissa. I think I just want to.

MELISSA

Then I shall marry the squirrel.

DUKE

And I shall marry the hag.

VALENCIO

Alas, there is no one for me to marry.

PORKS

'Tis true. Now I feel sorry for
Valencio. I shall marry Valencio
instead.

SHOE SALESMAN

But now I'm left out.

PORKS

Then I shall marry Melissa as I first
intend'd. And Valencio shall marry thee,
shoe salesman, 'tis fit.

DUKE

'Tis fit indeed. And now all we need is a
last line for our story.

MELISSA

Yes, truly this whole affair hath been
much ado about nothing.

SHOE SALESMAN

A real comedy of errors, thou might say.

VALENCIO

In life you must taketh the rough with the
smooth.
A little here, a little there; as you like it.

HAG

For life is truly a comedy of erro—
oh, we've already done that one.

PORKS

I see it falls to me to come up with
the perfect last line. Let me see. Well,
ev'ryone shall married be, so things hath
worked out fine. All's well that ends well.

SQUIRREL

    Fie! Not quite ev'ryone shall married be.

    For I have been left all alone in the world,

    with not even a nut to mine name.

    'Tis rubbish being a squirrel.

Exeunt, dancing and throwing flowers all over the place and the Squirrel nibbling some of them but not looking very happy about it.

FIN

The Witchfinder General

1.

Where had she come from, with her ragged cloak and her brass-buckled boots black as midnight? Where had she come from, with her tall pointy hat covered with cobwebs, and spiders dangling from the brim?

Where had she come from, with her cauldron, and her jar of scorpions clutched in one hand and her broomstick in the other and her black cat, Bad Luck Graham, hissing and spitting upon her shoulder, and her imps and demons floating all around her and her toads and newts hopping about her feet, and her weird chin shaped like a coat hook and her bumpy old nose all spotted with pimples and warts and her dirty great book of spells under one withered arm?

Nobody knew where Strange Mildred had come from. All they knew is that she arrived at midnight on New Year's Day, by the light of a blood-red moon.

2.

'Have you met our new neighbour yet?' said rosy-cheeked Prudence Cobb, the baker, as she busied herself with the customers one morning. 'She's moved in to that ramshackle hut down by the Lamonic River, the one with all the bats and the strange shrieking sounds. She seems ever so nice.'

'She came into my shop the other day,' replied Eliza Bartlett, the dressmaker, 'looking for some needles and pins to stick in her "magic dolls", whatever they might be! Oh, and for some reason she wanted a lock of my hair. She's ever so friendly, don't you think so, Doctor Twigs?'

Doctor Twigs had been the town's physician for as long as anyone could remember. He always carried a large black bag full of rice, for as he was fond of saying, 'Look at my bag, it's full of rice.'

'Look at my bag, it's full of rice,' said Doctor Twigs. And that was all he had to say on the subject of Strange Mildred.

3.

If there was anything wrong in the little town of Lamonic Bibber that year, no one thought much of it, at least not to begin with. In February, little Barney Borley, playing down by the riverside, suddenly found that he had grown the legs of a hyena; but that was not uncommon in those days, and most people just put it down to something he ate.

Towards the end of March, Eliza Bartlett began waking at night with pricking pains all over her body. 'Exactly as if someone were stabbing me with needles and pins!' she exclaimed.

'It's only to be expected at your age,' replied Prudence Cobb, rolling out the dough with her big furry paws, which for some reason had replaced her hands only that morning. 'I'm sure you'll get over it soon.'

In June, Wallace Blackthorne found that his crops were failing, though the weather had been fine and the fields sown with plenty of time to spare.

'I never seen the likes of it,' he remarked over an ale at the Jugged Hare one lunchtime. 'What do you think, Doctor Twigs?'

'Look at my bag, it's full of rice,' said Doctor Twigs.

As the year drew on, the town's misfortunes grew. In August the water from the pump went bad. There was an outbreak of smallpox among the babies and an outbreak of slightlybiggerpox amongst the toddlers. The cows stopped giving their milk, the chickens stopped laying their eggs and the pigs stopped producing their delicious organic honey. A dog called Thimbles began barking backwards and a toadstool that looked a bit like the Devil's never-you-mind was found growing in the Old Meadow.

Eventually, Elmer Goodfellow, the town mayor, decided that something ought to be done. So one September evening, when the bonfires were burning in the fields, he called a meeting in the Town Hall and asked everyone to attend.

5.

'Friends,' said Elmer Goodfellow, looking out over the sea of anxious faces before him. 'Lamonic Bibber has faced many troubles in its time, but this year has been the worst in living memory. Our crops are failing, our children are getting all sorts of different-sized poxes and Thimbles keeps going "!KRAB !FOOW !FOOW !FOOW !KRAB"'

Elmer Goodfellow paused to let his words and backwards dog impressions set in. Then he took a candle and held it under his chin to make what he was about to say next even more dramatic and spooky.

'Such ill fortune cannot be natural, friends,' whispered Elmer Goodfellow. 'Methinks – ouch – someone in this – ouch, I wish I hadn't done this thing with the candle, it's burning my chin

– methinks – ouch – someone in this town is not what they appear to be. Friends and neighbours, methinks there walks amongst us . . . a witch!'

At this, all pretence of calm was lost and the townsfolk flew into a horrified uproar.

'A witch?' cried Wallace Blackthorne.

'We're doomed!' wailed Prudence Cobb.

'Look at my bag, it's full of rice,' said Doctor Twigs.

'Friends! Friends!' said Elmer Goodfellow, calling for quiet by rapping upon the lectern with a small wooden gavel, which is a type of small gavel made of wooden. 'We must keep our wits about us. Yes – Gareth Hustings, the fishmonger's boy? You have a question?'

'Aye,' said Gareth Hustings, a spotty but

sensible lad. 'Is it really all that difficult to spot a witch? I mean, wouldn't it be quite obvious?'

'Nay,' said Elmer Goodfellow gravely. 'You see, witches are masters at blending in amongst ordinary folk, and they look as normal as you or I. In fact,' he continued, 'any one of us here tonight could be the witch. It could be a woman, or a man, or a child. Or even a kettle, no, actually forget that, the witch couldn't be a kettle. Sorry, I don't know what I was thinking, I'm just a bit stressed out by this whole situation. The witch definitely isn't a kettle.'

'Are you sure?' said Henry Eames, the miller, eyeing a large copper kettle in the corner of the room.

'Yes, I'm positive,' said Elmer Goodfellow. 'Look around! Look around at thy friends and thy families and thy neighbours! Any one of us could be the witch, I tell you!'

'But definitely not the kettle?' said Henry Eames.

'Definitely not the kettle,' said Elmer Goodfellow firmly. 'One hundred per cent not the kettle. Really, Henry, forget about the kettle. I'm sorry I mentioned it.'

The townsfolk peered suspiciously at one another in the yellowish gloom. These were people they had known their whole life, people they saw every day! But now each face seemed unfamiliar and strange. Mothers looked at their sons as if seeing them for the first time. Sisters regarded their little brothers with horror, I mean even more horror than usual. Henry Eames looked at the kettle again, just in case.

'If only there were some easy way to spot witches,' sighed Elmer Goodfellow.

7.

Throughout the meeting, Strange Mildred had been sitting at the back of the hall in her pointed hat and her cloak and her boots, wrapped in a haze of foul-smelling purple smoke, her black cat perched on her shoulder as she stirred her cauldron with an old horse bone, whispering, *'Kill them all! One by one! Mix the potions! Tum-ti-tum!'* But now she raised one of her twisted, claw-like hands and spoke up.

'I got sumfink to say,' she croaked, coughing up a spider and a couple of worms.

'Ah,' said Elmer Goodfellow fondly. ''Tis Strange Mildred, the mysterious crone who came to live in our town a few months ago, exactly when these troubles began. Strange Mildred, who never meant a living soul any trouble in all her days.'

'Good old Strange Mildred,' agreed everyone. 'She really is a normal person and has cheered up the whole community.'

'She is so much fun! She lives next door to me and she is always doing magic tricks!'

grunted a four-year-old boy through his brand-new snout.

'What was it you wanted to say, Strange Mildred?' said Elmer Goodfellow. 'You have the floor, whatever that means.'

Strange Mildred stood up and addressed the hall.

'A curse on you, a curse on you all!' she began. 'May yer skin rot off an' yer hair fall out an' all yer livestock starve to death!'

'What a character,' laughed Eliza Bartlett.

'Right then,' continued Strange Mildred, picking a mushroom out of her nose and flicking it at a nearby baby. 'I nearly keeled over dead of boredom listenin' to you lot goin' on an' on. If you ask me, none of you's got 'alf a brain between ya. Wot we need's a Witchfinder General, that'll sort things out quick smart.'

'An excellent idea!' cried Elmer Goodfellow. 'All in favour of appointing a Witchfinder General, say aye.'

'Aye,' the shout went up.

'Look at my bag, it's full of rice,' added Doctor Twigs.

8.

''Tis decided then,' said Elmer Goodfellow. 'A Witchfinder General we want, and a Witchfinder General we shall have. Yes, a Witchfinder General, that's the thing. We must have a Witchfinder General! So that's definite then, we've voted and we can't go back on it. Now, Strange Mildred,' he continued, 'could you please explain what it is that a Witchfinder General actually does? None of us have the foggiest.'

'Certainly,' cackled Strange Mildred. 'A Witchfinder General is a person wot goes around accusin' people of being witches an' then drowns 'em. It's very simple, really – loads of chuckin' people in the pond, 'undreds of drowned bodies, no witches . . . Bingo! Problem solved.'

'That sounds absolutely ideal,' said Elmer Goodfellow – and then a thought struck him. 'Would *you* like to be the Witchfinder General, Strange Mildred? Seeing as it was your idea?'

'It'd be my pleasure,' grinned Strange Mildred, tossing a few phantoms into the cauldron. '*Spoil the milk! Weevils in the bread! Off wiv the fat little farmer boy's head!* I'll soon sniff that witch out all right, they got no chance!'

'Well, that's settled then,' said Elmer

Goodfellow. 'Would anyone else like to say anything – no, NOT you, Doctor Twigs.'

9.

And so it was that Strange Mildred was appointed the first Witchfinder General of Lamonic Bibber. She was given an office right next to the Town Hall (in fact she took over Elmer Goodfellow's office and he had to conduct his business from a haystack), and a big shiny badge, and special permission to go into people's houses and poke them with a stick and shout, 'ARE YOU A WITCH? WELL, ARE YOU? ARE YOU? ARE YOU?' until they started crying and saying things like, 'I don't know, it's . . . What's going on? Please, leave me be, it's three o'clock in the morning!'

And then Strange Mildred would pounce.

'Aha! Whatcha doin' up at three in the mornin'? Only witches gets up at three in the mornin', cos that's when they like to do their spells.'

'But, Strange Mildred, it was you who woke me in the first pla—'

'None of yer excuses! Or do you want anuvver poke wiv me stick?'

'Please! Leave me be! I was having a lovely dream about porridge.'

'Aha!' Strange Mildred would cry. 'That seals it, that does. Dreams about porridge, is it? Only witches has them dreams, that's well known, that is!'

'But –'

'No buts! You're a witch, ain'tcha? A stinkin' old witch! Bad Luck Graham, arrest this un-nacheral fiend!'

And then Bad Luck Graham would drag the unfortunate victim into the town square, still half-asleep and sobbing with terror, and Strange Mildred would cry, 'Quick, everyone! I found another one! This one's even worse than the last!'

Before September was out, nearly a hundred 'witches' had been arrested and locked up in the Town Hall, where they were fed twice a week on bread and water. By the time October rolled around, the number was almost double that.

'What are you going to do with them all?' asked Elmer Goodfellow as he sat in the Witchfinder General's office one morning, watching her eat her breakfast.

'I'm gonna wait 'til 'Alloween, ain't I?' replied Strange Mildred, crunching into a beetle.

'Then I'm gonna chuck 'em all in the pond.'

'Is that really necessary?' said Elmer Goodfellow.

'Course it's necessary, fatso,' said Strange Mildred. 'I told ya, you gotta drown them witches, it's the only fing for it. Drown 'em up, every last one of 'em! *"Drowny, drowny, drowny, drowny, drown, drown, drown!"* That's my motto.'

'That's a horrible motto,' said the mayor. 'And, well, it's just that – there does seem to be an awful lot of witches. You've arrested nearly everyone in town.'

'Yeah, that's the way it goes sometimes,' agreed Strange Mildred. 'You start lookin' for witches an' you find there's loads more than wot you fort. It's a shame, but there we are. Way fings is goin', I reckon I'm just gettin' started, an' all.'

'But –'

'No buts,' said Strange Mildred. 'You wanted a Witchfinder General, din'tcha? Well, now you've got one, ain'tcha?'

'But –'

'I'm gettin' tired of you,' said Strange Mildred. 'Graham, arrest this witch at once, 'e's stinkin' up the place.'

'I'm not a witch!' cried Elmer Goodfellow as the horrid and unusually powerful little cat dragged him off, kicking and screaming. 'I'm not a witch, I tell you!'

'Well done, Graham,' said Strange Mildred, once the cat had returned. ''Ere, I whipped you up yer favourite treat – mouse juice.'

'Thank you, mistress,' said Bad Luck Graham. 'Very kind.'

'Graham! I din't know you could talk!' exclaimed Strange Mildred. 'We known each other for two 'undred years, an' all this time you jus' been miaowin' an' purrin' an' that.'

'Well, I never had anything I particularly wanted to say before,' replied Bad Luck Graham. 'But it just occurred to me – why do we want to drown everyone in town? I mean, what's in it for us?'

'Promotion, that's wot,' grinned Strange Mildred, her eyes shiny with greed and slugs. 'You turn a farmer into a pumpkin, or bump off a couple of milkmaids, an' no one pays a blind bit of attention, do they? But you get rid of a *whole town* . . . Well, then, yer in the money, ain'tcha? That'll get ya noticed, that will. More powers, a bigger hat – an' a certificate from the ruler of the witches, Queen 'Ecate 'erself.

Maybe even a fluffier tail for you, Graham. Wot do you fink of that?'

'Miaow,' said Bad Luck Graham, and he went back to lapping at his bowl.

10.

Halloween, and a bad moon rising.

Halloween, and the houses standing empty and unlit.

Halloween, and a cold mist turning everything to secrets and shadows.

Halloween.

'This is it,' whispered Strange Mildred, shivering deliciously in the cold night air, her cloak trailing out behind her, her boot heels clacking on the cobblestones like coffin nails being pounded in to those boxes you bury people in, what are they called again, I can't remember. 'This is the night wot we been waitin' for, Graham. This is our time.'

Bad Luck Graham purred and did that thing cats do where they sort of walk through your legs rubbing themselves against your shins with their tail all up and then turn round and immediately do it again, no one knows why.

Clack, clack, clack. Purr, purr, purr. And so they made their way to the Town Hall. Strange Mildred turned the key in the lock and flung the doors wide open, and there they all were, the good townsfolk of Lamonic Bibber. Half-starved. Chained to one another with heavy iron shackles. Throwing their hands out in their wretchedness and their woe.

'Let us be!' begged Eliza Bartlett. 'Let us be! I mean, set us free first, obviously, it's horrible being chained up in a Town Hall. But then – let us be!'

'Pray mercy on us all!' cried Wallace Blackthorne. 'Or if you can't manage mercy on us all, how about just on me?'

'Mercy!' cried the townsfolk. 'Mercy!'

'No mercy,' grinned Strange Mildred, 'not for a rotten bunch of witch-faces like you.'

'Do you know?' whispered Elmer Goodfellow, as Strange Mildred took up the chain and led them out into the misty October night. 'I'm starting to think that maybe Strange Mildred was the witch all along.'

'Do you think so?' frowned Prudence Cobb. 'Strange Mildred? No, not her, I shan't believe it.'

'Shut yer traps,' sneered Strange Mildred, giving Elmer Goodfellow a cuff round the head and an extra-hard yank on the chain. Oh, what a sorry sight those townsfolk were, being dragged along the winding streets like cattle to the slaughter, and with barely the strength to take the next step. But each time someone stumbled or fell, Bad Luck Graham was upon them in a trice, scritching and scratching at their ankles until they were back on their feet and shambling along once more.

At last they reached the pond on the town green.

The water glimmered in the silvery moonlight.

A strange electricity seemed to fill the air.

It was time.

Bad Luck Graham got out his accordion and Strange Mildred started to sing her biggest ever hit, 'Down, Down, Down'.

'*Down, down, down!*' she sang.
'*Make the townsfolk drown!*
Down, down they go!
To the depths below!'

'Come on, you lot! Get into the spirit of it, sing along!' said Strange Mildred, who was having a fine old time of it, clicking her fingers and twirling about all over the place. 'No? All right, be like that, ya miserable lot!'

'*Down, down, down!*
Make the townsfolk drown!
Down, down they –'

But at that moment, a cloud passed in front of the moon and someone came round the corner, whistling softly.

11.

For a moment, the figure just stood there. Then he – or she, it was hard to tell in the darkness – strode up to Strange Mildred and tapped her firmly on the shoulder.

'Eh?' said Strange Mildred, whirling around quick as a hornets' eye. 'Wot's goin' on?'

The townsfolk looked on, holding their breath, hardly daring to hope. Could this be the hero they had been waiting for?

'Wot's goin' on?' demanded Strange Mildred again.

Slowly, the dark figure raised one hand. There was something clutched in that hand, some menacing, bulky thing.

'Look . . .' said the dark figure.

Strange Mildred gulped. She took an uneasy step back, towards the pond.

'Look . . .' said the dark figure again.

Strange Mildred gulped again and took another step back.

'Look . . .' said the dark figure once more.

Strange Mildred gulped again and –

Just then the moon came back out and all was revealed.

'Look at my bag, it's full of rice,' said Doctor Twigs.

'Oh, for goodness' sake,' groaned the townsfolk, clutching their heads in their hands. Strange Mildred stood there in astonishment – and then she broke into helpless peals of laughter.

'Wot?' she laughed. 'Did you fink it was some magic 'ero come to rescue you or sumfink? Wot is even wrong wiv this town, I ask ya?'

Without so much as a further glance,

Strange Mildred batted Doctor Twigs aside, and the poor fellow went sprawling. The black bag flew from his grasp and sunk like a stone beneath the waters of the pond.

'Bunch of eejits,' muttered Strange Mildred. 'Drownin's too good for 'em, if you ask me.'

'Then maybe don't do it?' suggested Wallace Blackthorne hopefully.

'Too late!' screamed Strange Mildred. And so saying, she gave Elmer Goodfellow a sudden hard shove in the small of the back.

'NOOOOOO!' cried Elmer Goodfellow as he tumbled into the pond, not for fear of his own life, but for the lives of his beloved friends and neighbours.

'NOOOOOO!' cried Elmer Goodfellow as the heavy iron chains dragged the rest of the townsfolk after him.

'NOOOOOO!' cried Elmer Goodfellow as his head disappeared beneath the water.

And maybe he did a few more 'NOOOOOO!'s after that, but if he did, I don't know, because he was underwater and I couldn't hear him. I can't tell you what people say when they're underwater, it's impossible.

The little pond bubbled and boiled with the thrashings of the townsfolk, like something from a fever dream. Legs, arms, faces, hands clawing frantically at the air – all appeared and disappeared once more. Heads bobbed up for a moment and sunk back down as the townsfolk tried to somehow not be in a pond even though they were in a pond –

And then suddenly the waters were still.

12.

'We done it, we done it!' shrieked Strange Mildred, catching up Bad Luck Graham's front paws in her bony old hands and dancing round and round with him in the moonlight.

Round and round and round they danced, as the town clock struck midnight. Round and round, faster and faster, faster and faster and round and round, and the clock bells tolled as they jigged and whirled, and as they danced a swamp-green mist came up between the pair of them and now a shape was materializing in that mist, a tall and terrible shape . . .

It was Hecate, Queen of the Witches.

'Cease your nonsense, Mildred,' commanded Queen Hecate, and each word she spoke was like a dagger in the night, cold and shiny and hard as tempered steel.

'Queen 'Ecate, yer royal 'ighness,' said Strange Mildred, bowing so low that her long nose went worming across the ground, where it was instantly attacked by an owl. 'Queen 'Ecate! Guess what I done, Queen 'Ecate?'

'Do tell, Mildred,' said Queen Hecate, stifling a yawn.

'I drowned up an 'ole town in one go,' said Mildred proudly. 'Yep, you 'eard me right – an 'ole town! You gotta give me a promotion now, ain'tcha? I wanna be the most powerful witch ever. An' I want a new cauldron. An' a better wand an' all, the one I got's absolutely pants. Oh, an' a bigger an' uglier nose to scare people wiv, my nose ain't quite big enough as it is, an' besides, an owl just bit quite a lot of it off. An'–'

'Where exactly did you carry out this

spectacular drowning?' asked Queen Hecate with a sigh.

'Where'dya fink?' said Strange Mildred. 'I done it in that pond over there, see?'

'What, that pond right there?' said Queen Hecate. 'The one that's full of happy, smiling, completely un-drowned people?'

'Yup,' said Strange Mildred triumphantly, 'that's – oh. 'Ow did that 'appen?'

'Do you know what happens to dried rice in water, Mildred?' sighed Queen Hecate. 'The rice absorbs the water, Mildred, that's what happens. And then the rice expands, Mildred, that's what happens. And when the rice expands, it rises up in a great heap, Mildred, that's what happens.'

'Oh,' said Strange Mildred in a small voice. 'Is that why – is that why, um, all them people wot I drowned din't actually drown an' is sittin' on a big fluffy mountain of rice laughin' an' gigglin' an', um, doin' raspberries at me?'

'Precisely, Mildred,' said Queen Hecate.

'Oh,' said Strange Mildred.

'Bye bye, Mildred,' yawned Queen Hecate. She blinked once and Strange Mildred winked out of existence with a tiny little 'pop'. Then Queen Hecate blinked again and Bad Luck Graham turned into an onion and went drifting away on the breeze. And that is why, to this day, onions have nine lives.

Then Queen Hecate turned towards the townsfolk and – blink! – their chains melted away like smoke and – blink! – all of the magic animal tails and fur and stuff that Strange Mildred had done on them vanished in one go and – blink! – that one wasn't a magic blink, Queen Hecate just needed to blink.

'I'm sorry you had to see me dealing with my employee like that,' said Queen Hecate. 'But I can't stand bad witchcraft – and Strange Mildred was simply the worst. You're free to go, every one of you. Happy Halloween, Lamonic Bibber!'

With one last blink she was gone and the townsfolk were left there, sitting on their mountain of rice in the moonlight, gaping in amazement and trying to make sense of it all.

'Well, Doctor Twigs, it looks like we are forever indebted to you,' said Elmer Goodfellow, when he had finally recovered his wits. 'You've saved the entire town!'

'Look at the pond, it's full of rice,' said Doctor Twigs.

And that was all he had to say on the subject.

13.

Where had she come from, with her little hunched back and her dry old mouth with only one black tooth left in it and when you looked at it, it made you feel sick? Where had she come from, with her plans and her schemes and her fingernails sharp as knives and her flashing yellow eyes? Where had she come from, with her chants and her potions and her evil as old as time? No one knew where Peculiar Edith had come from. All they knew is that she arrived a few days after Halloween, riding in a carriage of dead men's bones.

'Have you met our new neighbour?' said rosy-cheeked Prudence Cobb, handing Eliza Bartlett a fresh-baked loaf. 'Ever so friendly. And makes herself useful, I should say! She's down at the pond right now, helping them clear out the rice.'

The End

Lord Famous and The Plague

It was a Wednesday afternoon in the middle of the seventeenth century when it all began. A famous lord called Lord Famous was lying around in his parlour having a live stag stuffed down his throat by his servants, when in rushed a messenger, so red in the face that at first Lord Famous thought he was an enormous cherry on legs. Enormous cherries on legs were quite common in those days, so it was an easy enough mistake to make.

Immediately Lord Famous jumped up, wiped an antler from his lips, and popped the messenger's head into his mouth. He was about to bite it in half to get at the lovely cherry juice inside but luckily his servant, a wise fellow by the name of Fiddle-Me-Riddle-Me-Buckler, spoke up just in time.

'Lord Famous,' said Fiddle-Me-Riddle-Me-Buckler. 'That is not an enormous cherry on legs, it is a messenger, spit him out at once.'

So Lord Famous spat out the red-faced messenger, who collapsed on the floor in a heap of other red-faced messengers that Lord Famous had recently tried to eat, thinking that they too were enormous cherries on legs.

'Hello,' said the messenger, getting up and wiping the spit from his eyes, his face redder than ever. 'I am a –'

But before he could continue, Lord Famous had pounced on him and was trying to eat him once more. That was the thing about Lord Famous – he loved enormous cherries on legs, and also he never learned from his mistakes.

'Lord Famous!' shouted Fiddle-Me-Riddle-Me-Buckler. 'Spit that young man out, for he is no cherry, as I told you before!'

'Oh, yes,' said Lord Famous, spitting out the messenger again. 'All right. Now, what is it you have run these many miles to tell? What could be so important that you would come in here and disturb my luncheon?'

To be honest, it was difficult *not* to disturb Lord Famous's luncheon, as it lasted from six o'clock in the morning until 5.58 the next morning. He was always eating and he would eat anything he could get his mouth on – stags, geese, porcupines, a horse that had fallen over by the side of the road, walnuts, all sorts of things. Once he had invented a massive tube, about three hundred miles long, which he would hold to his mouth. Then he'd point the other end into the air and just suck birds out of the sky and swallow them whole. He really was quite a greedy man, not the greediest in the country perhaps, but definitely in the top twenty. In between his luncheons, Lord Famous had two minutes in which to sleep, go to the toilet, write his memoirs, hang people for being poor and talk to his wife. So it wasn't very easy being a lord in those days, as you can see. There were all sorts of things to do and hardly any time to do them in, and all because of luncheon.

'What could be so important that you would come in here and disturb my luncheon?' repeated Lord Famous now. 'Or,' he added hopefully, 'are you in fact not a messenger at all, but instead an enormous cherry on legs?'

Lord Famous opened his mouth wide once more but luckily the messenger spoke up in the nick of time.

'Lord Famous,' said the messenger. 'I bring bad tidings from London town. Men are dropping in the streets. Women are dropping in the streets. Children are dropping in the streets. Everyone is dropping in the streets, it is dreadful and quite noisy. And the reason,

Lord Famous, is a plague, yes, a horrible plague, which is sweeping that fair city.'

'How does it spread?' bellowed Lord Famous so loudly that his wig flew off, shot out the window and exploded in a nearby field.

'It is spread by rats and fleas,' said the messenger. 'They carry the plague inside their bodies and do you know why? It is because they hate people and want to take over the world.'

'Stupid rats and fleas,' said Lord Famous. 'Well, thanks for telling me about the plague, but if it's all the way down in London what harm can it do us here?'

But the messenger uttered not another word, for he had suddenly died of the plague. He had bright purple boils all over his face and neck, and there were dozens of rats and fleas running all over him. And now Lord Famous

trembled, for his house had become not just a House of Luncheon – but a House of Luncheon and Horrible Plague.

'Fiddle-Me-Riddle-Me-Buckler!' cried Lord Famous. 'What are we to do?'

But Fiddle-Me-Riddle-Me-Buckler uttered not a word, because he too had suddenly died of the plague and was lying there covered in his own boils and rats and fleas.

'Never mind,' said Lord Famous, 'Fiddle-Me-Riddle-Me-Buckler wasn't a very good character anyway. I'd better see how my wife's doing, though,' he added. 'I quite like her.'

Lord Famous heaved his enormous fat body upstairs and went into his wife's bedroom.

'Wife,' said he. 'A horrible plague has

descended upon this house and I want to see if you're all right.'

'I am fine,' said his wife, who was sitting up in the four-poster-bed doing a crossword.

'Good,' said Lord Famous. 'How's your crossword going?'

But his wife uttered not another word, for she had suddenly died of the plague after all and her face cracked open and hundreds of fleas and rats ran out from behind it and jumped up and down on the bed, grinning. Yes, grinning.

'I hate the plague,' said Lord Famous, going back downstairs. 'I'd better see what time it is, even though it's not that important and doesn't really follow on from my last sentence.'

Lord Famous glanced at the magnificent clock on the parlour wall but it had died of the plague as well and was covered in rats and fleas.

Lord Famous picked up a rat and shook it to see if gold would come out of it. None did, but it never hurts to try looking on the bright side of things.

'I'd better see what's happening outside, because everyone in here's dead and to be honest it's a bit depressing,' said Lord Famous. He opened the front door with his mind, which is how people opened their front doors in those days. Then he stepped outside with his legs, which is how people stepped outside in those days, a tradition which has continued into the modern age.

It was a lovely sunny day. Across the fields, Lord Famous could see children playing a game of hoopy-cockles. Hoopy-cockles was a delightful seventeenth-century game. Each child is given a colourful wooden hoop decorated

with bows and ribbons. Then they roll the
hoops down the hill and up again, singing:

Hoopy-cockles! Hoopy-cockles!
Mustard seed and hollyhock!
Hoopy-cockles! Hoopy-cockles!
Peaseblossom! Peaseblossom!
Hoopy-cockles! Hoopy-cockles!
Mustard seed and hollyhock!
Jack-in-the-hedge!
Jack-in-the-hedge!
In the merry month of May!

'Ah, hoopy-cockles,' sighed Lord Famous,
wiping a tear from his eye. 'I remember how
as a child I would play that game. I never knew
what those words meant, but they always made
me feel that life was worth living and that it

was fun to push a wooden hoop down a hill and back up again.'

Lord Famous cast his gaze in another direction, and saw a lovely old lady walking her pheasant, a proud bird indeed by the name of Pembroke.

He looked in another direction and saw a pretty milkmaid milking a smiling cow by turning on its special taps.

He looked in another direction and saw a tiny lamb being tickled by buttercups.

He looked in another direction and saw a happy mother pushing a pram filled with laughing newborn piglets.

He looked in another direction and saw a handsome young gentleman kissing his sweetheart's knees.

He looked in another direction and saw a

juggler making everyone smile.

He looked in another direction and saw an enormous cherry on legs, a real one this time.

He looked in another direction and saw a fox ripping the head off a hen.

'Life is so beautiful,' said Lord Famous. 'Although I wish I hadn't looked in that last direction, that one wasn't so nice.'

And it was then that Lord Famous realised something.

'All my life I have been selfish and thought only about luncheon,' said Lord Famous. 'I have never taken the time to appreciate the simple, everyday folk. Just look at all these innocent people and animals and enormous cherries on legs. I cannot let the plague spread to the rest of Lamonic Bibber. If I am to act, it must be now!'

Never a truer word had been uttered, for

even now the first of the fleas was hopping out of Lord Famous's front door and starting across the fields. And behind the flea, a rat was emerging from the shadows.

'It is time,' said Lord Famous. 'Time for my last – and greatest – luncheon of all.'

Lord Famous heaved himself over to the flea and in one swift movement, he gobbled it up. Then he ate the rat. Then he ate another rat that was coming out of the house behind the first rat. Then he ate some fleas that were behind the second rat. Then he ate some more rats and some more fleas and another couple of rats and some more fleas and – well, you get the picture, Lord Famous munched his way through an awful lot of rats and fleas that day, and although it was hard going he did not once waver in his duty. Eventually, after about four hours straight of wobbling through the house eating rats and fleas, Lord Famous sat back in his parlour, his large stomach heaving.

'Ooh,' said Lord Famous, wiping his brow with an old rag. 'I feel as sick as a dog.'

And that is where we get the phrase, 'wiping his brow with an old rag'.

Lord Famous knew the end was near. He rolled over onto his back and lay gazing weakly up at the parlour ceiling.

'I do not ask to be remembered as a hero,' he announced, 'nor celebrated with great buildings and research institutes in my name. By preventing the spread of this ghastly plague, I have done the right thing – that is all. And now I die, happy in the knowledge that the good men, women, children, piglets, cows, pheasants and cherries of my hometown are safe.'

With these noble words, Lord Famous died, and with his death the plague came to an end. He was truly a remarkable man, perhaps one of the greatest citizens the town of Lamonic Bibber has ever known.

The next day another plague came to Lamonic Bibber, even worse than the first one, and everyone else died too.

THE END

The
GREAT FIRE

IT WAS ONLY A YEAR since the plague had wiped
out *everyone in town*, but the streets of
Lamonic Bibber were as full of life as ever.
Where had these *new settlers* come from?
Maybe they'd moved there from the nearby
villages and towns. Perhaps they'd just sort
of grown out of the ground, like eagles do.
However it had happened, the town was fit to
bursting, with all sorts of friendly folk going

about their seventeenth-century business in the NARROW LANES FULL OF HIGHLY FLAMMABLE RUBBISH that lay between the HIGGLEDY-PIGGLEDY, BADLY-BUILT WOODEN BUILDINGS which crowded in so close that the THATCHED ROOVES OF STRAW often touched one another.

'Ah, this is the safest town in the whole of England,' smiled Samuel Tulks, the EXTREMELY CLUMSY AND ABSENT-MINDED BAKER, as he wandered down the high street, SMOKING A BIG PIPE. Everyone in those days SMOKED BIG PIPES and they were always DROPPING HUNKS OF SMOULDERING TOBACCO EVERYWHERE THEY WENT.

'It certainly is,' replied Robert Greaves, the GUNPOWDER MERCHANT, who was walking at Samuel's side, PLAYING WITH MATCHES. 'Do you know, I was just talking to George Carlisle, the BLACKSMITH, the other day. We were standing in his INCREDIBLY HOT AND DANGEROUS FORGE and he was HAMMERING AWAY AT SOME HOT METAL WITH HIS EYES SHUT AND MAKING SPARKS FLY EVERYWHERE, and he was saying as how nothing bad could ever happen here. Oh, I know there was some trouble with the plague last year, but that's all over now. The best days of Lamonic Bibber lie ahead of us, Samuel, mark my words!'

'I couldn't agree more,' replied Samuel contentedly. 'Oh, look, there's Bessie Bingles, who's always COOKING FOOD ON A LARGE UNSTABLE STOVE IN A TINY LITTLE PIE SHOP FULL OF STACKS OF

OLD NEWSPAPERS. Good day to you, Bessie.'

'Good day to you, gentlemen, good day indeed,' smiled Bessie Bingles. 'Would you mind doing me a favour? I've got a GIGANTIC BARREL OF COOKING OIL that needs delivering to old Parson Muffler down at the CHURCH THAT'S MADE ENTIRELY OF DRY STRAW AND KINDLING, right next door to that ENORMOUS PILE OF COAL THAT SOMEONE DUMPED IN THE STREET. Would you mind taking it?'

'Why, it would be our pleasure,' replied Samuel, who secretly fancied Mrs Bingles because he thought she was HOT, and who would have done anything to win her favour. 'Let's just ROLL THIS BARREL DOWN THE STREET EVEN THOUGH IT'S VERY LEAKY INDEED.

That will be the best way to
transport it.'

'A fine idea, a fine
idea indeed,' replied the

gunpowder merchant, and off they set.

'Ah! Mr Tulks! Mr Greaves! A good day to you, gentlemen,' exclaimed old Parson Muffler when they arrived at the church. 'I see you've brought me my cooking oil, how useful. Just put it in the back, by the altar, would you? That's it, directly underneath all those SPUTTERING CANDLES WHICH ARE CONSTANTLY DRIPPING HOT WAX ALL OVER THE PLACE, that's perfect. Now, can I interest either of you in a drop of EXTRA-STRONG WHISKY?'

'I shouldn't really, it's a bit early for me,' said Samuel, 'but – oh, go on then, naughty!'

'I'll take a snifter too,' said Robert. 'Don't mind if I do.'

'There you go, gents,' said old Parson Muffler. 'Oops, I've POURED MOST OF THE

BOTTLE ALL OVER YOUR CLOTHES. I'm dreadfully sorry, my eyesight isn't what it used to be.'

'Think nothing of it,' said Samuel, reaching into his pocket for a BURNING TAPER to light everyone's pipes. 'Ah, this is the life. Well, we must be on our way, Parson. We've some business to discuss with Isaac Croft down by the RICKETY WOODEN DOCKS.'

'Send Isaac my regards,' said old Parson Muffler as the pair set off. 'And would you mind giving him this? It's a FLAMING TORCH MADE FROM A PLANK WRAPPED IN RAGS DOUSED IN BOILING SHEEP FAT.'

'No problem whatsoever,' said Robert. 'I'll BALANCE IT PRECARIOUSLY ON MY HEAD. That will be the best way to carry it, even though it's SPITTING GLOBS OF HOT

SIZZLING FAT IN EVERY DIRECTION.'

Soon Samuel and Robert had come to Isaac Croft's FIREWORKS IMPORTING COMPANY down by the docks. Big SPLINTERY CRATES OF ROMAN CANDLES, ROCKETS AND JUMPING JACKS lay in untidy profusion, SPILLING THEIR CONTENTS OVER THE SAWDUST-STREWN FLOOR.

'Good day, gentlemen, good day,' said Isaac. 'Do come in, I was just MESSING ABOUT WITH THESE CHINESE FIRECRACKERS. I was LIGHTING THEM AND SEEING HOW FAR ACROSS THE WAREHOUSE I COULD FLICK THEM. Would you like to join me?'

'Certainly,' replied Samuel Tulks, and the three men passed a pleasant hour or two engaged in this fine sport.

'Now, what did you want to see me about?'

asked Isaac presently.

'Oh, yes,' said Samuel. 'I was wondering if you could sell me HUNDREDS AND HUNDREDS OF SPARKLERS. I've got an eye-catching new idea for my bakery. I thought it would be nice to STICK LIT SPARKLERS IN THE TOPS OF MY CAKES to attract the attention of passers-by.'

'And I'd like to buy some CATHERINE WHEELS,' said Robert. 'I thought it would bring more business into my gunpowder shop if I had a display of HUNDREDS OF CATHERINE WHEELS SPINNING IN THE SHOP WINDOW, PRODUCING SPARKS THAT COULD LAND SIMPLY ANYWHERE.'

'An excellent notion!' cried Isaac, jumping up at once and hunting around in the back of the factory. 'How many would you like?'

'About two thousand of each type,' said Samuel, 'that ought to do it. How much do we owe you, Isaac?'

'Sixpence,' replied Isaac. 'I know it's quite cheap but it's the Old Days. Also, some of these fireworks are A BIT FAULTY AND COULD BLOW UP WHEN YOU LIGHT THEM. Do you need a bag?'

'No, no,' said Samuel. 'We'll just carry them STICKING OUT OF OUR POCKETS EVERY WHICH WAY. See you later for the BIG BONFIRE PARTY IN THE MIDDLE OF TOWN THAT WE HAVE EVERY SINGLE NIGHT OF THE YEAR, I hope?'

'I'll be there as usual, don't you worry,' laughed Isaac.

'What a nice chap,' said Samuel as

they walked back into town past the GLASSBLOWER'S, the MAGNIFYING GLASS SHOP THAT WAS ONLY OPEN ON SUNNY DAYS, the STANDS SELLING CHESTNUTS ROASTING ON OPEN BRAZIERS, some LITTLE GIRLS BANGING TWO ROCKS TOGETHER TO START A FIRE FOR LITERALLY NO REASON AT ALL and a SMALL CAT, SORRY, I DON'T KNOW WHY THIS ONE'S IN CAPITALS.

'Yes,' said Robert. 'And furthermore –'

But just then a newspaper boy ran up and pressed a copy of the Lamonical Chronicle into Samuel's hand.

'Read all about it! Read all about it!' cried the boy. 'Special edition!'

And off he sprinted down the street, TOSSING NEWSPAPERS LEFT, RIGHT

AND CENTRE.

Samuel scanned the front page.

'No!' he gasped. 'I don't – it's terrible! Oh, Robert, it seems there's been a Great Fire in London! Nearly half the city's burned down!'

'Well, they're awfully careless down there,' replied Robert, shaking his head disapprovingly as he TOYED WITH A LOADED MUSKET. 'If you ask me, it was an accident waiting to happen.'

THE END

Bibbering Through The Ages
Wednesday O'Leary

Wednesday O'Leary was the vicar of Lamonic Bibber between 1722 and 1745. A man of great learning, he could speak seven languages, although he had no idea what he was saying in any of them. He always wore two pairs of glasses, one on his eyes and one on the back of his head (so that he could see if any robins were chasing him) and he was fond of boasting that he could tell the difference between an armchair and a loaf of bread merely by eating them both and then guessing. He died in 1745 after trying to eat an armchair, and was buried in the ceiling of St Follican-in-the-Fields, the church to which he had devoted most of his adult

life. Although he died unmarried and without children, Wednesday O'Leary was the great-great-great-great-great grandfather of Friday O'Leary, who still lives in Lamonic Bibber today. And his hat was the great-great-great-great-great grandfather of Friday O'Leary's hat.

A FORK
IN THE
ROAD

Well now, if you doesn't know it I'll tell it an' if you does know it I'll tell it anyhow. Back in them days there was only one road in and out of Lamonic Bibber, an' a fearsome prospect it were too, most of it were unlit, you see – or rather, you don't see, because most of it were unlit. Yar, it were a dark road, so it were, an' it run through thick woods, so it did, an' the trees crowded in from all sides, loomin' over that road to make it even darker, so as you couldn't even see the stars and the moon, most likely. An' besides, back in them days the moon was all covered in trees an' all, so the moon weren't that bright even when you *could* see it, it were just a dark clump of trees in the sky. Course, nowadays all them trees on the moon's been cut down by the asternorts, what's a right shame – but that's the way of things, times change, so they do, yar.

So it were dark and lonesome, that road, and there was wild animals in them woods too – wolves an' worse things besides. But still,

247

back then it were the only road in an' out of Lamonic Bibber an' if you wanted to get out or in, that's how you did it. Only you didn't want to travel by night if you could help it – but sometimes you couldn't help it, like. Yar. Yar. That be the truth, yar. Sorry, I just really like sayin' 'yar'.

There was many occasions I heard of when bad things befell them what betravelled that road after dark, but the one I want to tell you about is what happened on January 24, 1780, when a woman name of Joanna Vale was returnin' to Lamonic Bibber by that route. Joanna had spent all day in the neighbourin' town of Wample-upon-Stample, visitin' her Great Uncle Tobacco who was sick in bed from tryin' to smoke his own surname, and she had sat at his bedside for hours without complaint, moppin' his fevered brow with a mop an' cryin' into his shoulder. For she were a kindly young lady, so she was, an' it were plain as day that her old uncs weren't long for this world. All day long Joanna sat there, her an' that doctor with her, old Doctor Twigs, who was a good man, true an' well-skilled in the art of medicine, an' together they done all they could. But eventually, with the rain lashin' down somethin' fierce outside the window, Great Uncle Tobacco turned his whiskery old face to Joanna an' croaked his final words.

'My dearest Joanna,' croaked he, 'I have lived a long and happy life. Let future generations know this: Life is for living, and for helping others and for spreading knowledge and love. COUGH COUGH COUGH COUGH COUGH PHLEGM COUGH PHLEGM COUGH.'

An' with that he passed from this world an' into the next.

'Such beautiful words,' sighed Joanna Vale. 'I shall have them engraved on his tombstone.'

An' indeed, even today you can read them words engraved on Great Uncle Tobacco's tombstone: 'COUGH COUGH COUGH COUGH COUGH PHLEGM COUGH PHLEM COUGH.'

Outside, the rain were comin' down harder than ever but inside the darkened room, all was still. Doctor Twigs pressed a couple of pennies down on old Tobacco's eyelids for to keep them ghosties away, an' pronounced the time of death as half past nine o' the clock o' the clock, yar, so he did, yar.

'Well, that is that,' said Doctor Twigs, taking Joanna's small, trembling hand in his own. 'Your great uncle was a fine man, Joanna, and you should be proud of him.'

'He was indeed,' said Joanna, battin' back a tear. 'But I am curious, Doctor. There was a Doctor Twigs in Lamonic Bibber many years ago, during the time of the Witchfinder General. Are you related to him?'

'No, no relation at all,' replied the doctor. 'Doctor Twigs is quite a common name for a doctor in these parts, you know. Now, what are your plans? Will you stay the night with me and Mrs Twigs, and return home to Lamonic Bibber with the body tomorrow morn?'

'Thank you,' replied Joanna Vale, 'but I should not think of imposing upon you and your wife. Call for a carriage – I shall travel back immediately.'

'What?' gasped Doctor Twigs. 'Surely you would not think of chancing the road on a night like this?'

But Joanna wouldn't be swayed, not even when Doctor Twigs set her on an enormous Swayin' Machine what he'd built and turned the settin' all the way up to 'Maximum Sway'. She stood her ground an' eventually Doctor Twigs saw that she was determined to start for home there and then. An' so he run through the rain to the nearest tavern, The Fox & Grapes, what they say dates back to Roman times, an' in he burst, him in his hat an' cloak an' umbrella, all drippin' with rain an' squirrels.

'Stephen!' cries Doctor Twigs to the barman. 'We need a carriage up at the Tobacco place. For old Tobacco himself is no more and his great niece intends to take the body back to Lamonic Bibber this very eve.'

'What?' cries Stephen, 'on a night like this? Will she not stay with you an' Mrs Twigs?'

'I offered,' says Doctor Twigs, 'but her mind is made up and she will not be swayed.'

'Have you tried her on that Swayin' Machine of yours?' says Stephen.

'I have,' replies Doctor Twigs.

'What, even on "Maximum Sway"?' says Stephen.

'Yes, yes,' cries Doctor Twigs impatiently, thumpin' his fist down on the bar so hard that – well, nothin' really happened but it was still quite a hard thump. 'She will not be swayed, I tell you.'

Well, at that, an old rummy by the name of Barnabus Tharnabus, who's sittin' all alone in the corner, speaks up.

'I don't likes the sound of this,' mutters old Barnabus, 'I seen strange things on that road at night. Strange things indeed.'

'Yes, we all know it's a terrible idea travelling on that road by night,' says Doctor Twigs, 'I think we've established that. But the long and the short of it is, the young lady wants a carriage and, if it is all right by you, a carriage she shall have.'

'Strange things,' says Barnabus. 'Terrible things.'

'I know,' says Doctor Twigs. 'I've tried to talk her out of it. I've tried the Swaying Machine and –'

''As you tried 'er on "Maximum Sway"?' says old Barnabus, downin' the last of his drink an' a-callin' for more.

'YES,' says Doctor Twigs. 'Now, Stephen, what say you? Have you a carriage ready to go or haven't you?'

'I have,' says Stephen the barkeep, darkly. 'But I'm with Barnabus. I don't like this. I don't like this one bit.'

'I don't like it either,' says Abigail Comely, who's sittin' in another corner of the tavern.

'Nor me,' says her friend, Janey Mallows. 'I don't care for it at all.'

'I KNOW,' says Doctor Twigs. 'Honestly, I totally get it. We're all in complete agreement but – look, just get me a carriage, will you?'

'Yar,' says Stephen the bartender, who quite liked sayin' 'yar' himself on occasion. 'I'll send Hemley, he's the only coachman brave enough to make a trip in such conditions as these.'

An' so a carriage was called for. Yar, so it were, yar, yar. Yar. Yar. Yarrity.

Now, what with all the talk down at the tavern, an' the business of wrappin' up Great Uncle Tobacco's body in a tablecloth an' gettin' it down the stairs into the front hall – it weren't until nearly eleven o' the clock o' the clock o' the clock that Joanna were all set an' ready to make the trip home. But when the stagecoach finally pulled up outside the house, Doctor Twigs' unease only grown more, for the man what sat upfront behind the reins were much taller an' thinner than Stephen's man, an' he were all done up in a jet black cloak an' his face half-hidden from view.

'Where's Hemley?' said the doctor. 'And who are you?'

'I am afraid Mr Hemley couldn't make it,' replied the coachman in a soft, still voice. 'I have been sent instead.'

'By whom?' demanded the doctor.

'I have been sent instead,' replied the coachman again. 'See here, my stagecoach is sturdy and its wheels are circular – the fastest of all the shapes. As for me, my eyes are keen and my hands are quite good at steering horses around corners. I am one of the best stagecoach drivers of all time, except I did once crash into a tree and kill all my passengers. But that probably won't happen again.'

'Who *are* you, though?' said Doctor Twigs.

But the coachman only smiled to himself an' turned away.

'I don't feel at all right about this,' said Doctor Twigs as he and Joanna loaded Great Uncle Tobacco's body onto the back seat. 'I shall sit up all night with worry.'

'I thank you for your concern,' said Joanna Vale. 'But there is nothing to fear. I shall be fine, I promise.'

Before Doctor Twigs could protest further, the mysterious stranger pulled on the reins and shouted them famous words, 'ANIMALS OF TRANSPORT, TAKE US ON OUR WAY!'

An' with that the carriage took off into the dark night, yar, yar, so it did. Yar.

Well now, if you doesn't know it I'll tell it an'

if you does know it I'll tell it anyhow. In them days the distance between Wample-upon-Stample an' Lamonic Bibber was sixty-two miles. Today the two towns is only forty-five miles apart cos of global warmin' – but that's the way, times change, yar, yar, yar, so they do, yar. Sixty-two full country miles it was back then, an' all on that one windin' road an' most of it through them dark, dark woods. Joanna couldn't barely see nothin' out the window, jus' them raindrops smashin' 'gainst the glass. The thunder crashed overhead an' the lightnin' lit up the sky from time to time, showin' the shapes of the trees all loomin'. An' the humped shape of her old uncs on the back seat an' all – oh, it were a fearful ride, so it was. Yar.

Onwards, onwards went the stagecoach, passin' the turn-offs for all them other towns an' villages what's in these parts: Little Flossingham, Wistrel-on-the-Hoof, Shambler Green, Asterly, Henry's Elbow . . .

'Are you sure we're going the right way?' Joanna asked the driver once. For though she had assured the doctor there was nothin' to

fear, the night was a-playin' on her nerves.

'How could we not be?' replied the driver, without turnin'. 'There is only one road, after all.'

On an' on they travelled, an' the driver whippin' them horses, whippin' 'em for their lives until the foam was frothin' at their mouths,

an' the night all mud an' water an' darkness an' the whole world turned to a bad, bad swirl, until Joanna begin to feel they been travellin' forever an' ever an' that they'd be goin' forever an' forever more.

At one point a little hill rose up to the side of the road an' on it a single crooked tree, all stunted an' horrible, no leaves, just them bare branches reachin' out, reachin' out like a screechin' man throwin' his arms up to the skies.

'I've never seen that place before,' says Joanna, a tiny tremor creepin' into her voice.

''Tis known as the Hill of Despair,' says the driver. 'And on it stands the Murder Tree. 'Tis said that once upon a time the Murder Tree was not a tree at all, but a bad man by the name of Ebeneezer Murder, who murdered his whole family with a spoon. And then he murdered himself with a spoon. And then he murdered an old lady with a spoon, just to see if he could still murder people after he'd murdered himself. And then – so they say – he was turned into that tree for his sins, his soul shrieking into the wind until the end of time.'

'Thank you, that's very reassuring,' says Joanna. An' she's about to say more, but suddenly the stagecoach come to a complete standstill in the middle of the road, yar.

'HALT, ANIMALS OF TRANSPORT!' cried the mysterious coachman, which were a bit pointless as the stagecoach had already come to a complete standstill. An' there it stayed, with the darkness all around an' the only sounds the beatin' of the rain on the carriage roof, an' the nervous tappin's of the horses's hooves on the gravel an' the scufflin's in the undergrowth – or mayhap that last one were just Joanna's mind a-playin' tricks.

'Driver,' says Joanna at length. 'Why have we stopped?'

For awhile he says nothin', just sits there upfront, one hand on the reins an' quiet as a stone. But then, slowly, silently, he gets down from his high seat an', comin' around the side of the carriage, he opens Joanna's door an' offers her his hand.

An' as if in a dream, Joanna takes that hand an' steps out into the lashin' rain.

'We have come to a fork in the road,' murmurs the driver in his soft, still voice.

'But that's impossible,' cries Joanna Vale, in a voice what she hardly recognises as her own. 'There is only one road, as everyone knows. You even said so yourself.'

'And yet there are many ways upon that road,' murmurs the driver. 'Many ways.'

An' now Joanna's heart misses a beat as she sees that there *is* a fork up ahead, one what was never there before. A fork in the road, standin' directly beneath a great tree – one of them great trees as used to be known in these parts as a Yingler der Splingler o' the Forest. To the right she can just make out the lights of her hometown. But on the left path, a ways off, she sees –

'Oh,' gasps Joanna Vale, fallin' to her knees in the rain. Cos what she saw then took her breath away in one instant. It were a city, so it were, yar, a city such as the world has never seen, all twisty spires an' impossible tall buildin's reachin' up into the sky an' all of it bathed in white light, so bright that it lit up the dark as if it were noon. An' the shapes of people – or mayhap not quite people – dancin' an' cavortin' in the streets an' on the rooftops, an' a music like none what she ever heard before, a strange music what seemed to be not of this world. An' if you ever chance to hear such music yourself, you'll know what I'm talkin' of, for it gets into your blood an' fills you with wild thoughts an' notions far beyond your everyday imaginin's.

'What is it?' breathes Joanna, so soft she's hardly aware she's even spoken.

'It is your final destination – if you so desire it, that is,' says the driver. 'A place where you can have whatever you want, anytime you wish. A place where every dream that ever you dreamt can come to pass, no matter how outlandish or unreal.'

'I –,' starts Joanna, but she can say no more,

just stands there as if in a dream.

'Choose, Joanna Vale,' whispers the driver. 'Choose your path. You need only say the word and all the wonders of that place will be yours.'

How long Joanna stood there I do not know. But it were like she was hypnotised by that city, that city pulsin' with its unearthly white light at the end of that left-hand path, an' she were unable to tear her gaze from it. An' yet she were torn inside, too, for it seemed like a fight were goin' on within her, all the things she knowed an' believed against all them things what might be waitin' for her in that new world.

'This is much harder than Doctor Twigs' Swaying Machine,' she moaned. 'Even on "Maximum Sway".'

'Say the word, Joanna Vale,' whispered the driver. 'Choose your path.'

Well, now, Joanna opened her mouth to answer – an' what she might of said just then, perhaps even she herself never knowed. But at that moment she sensed a movement from the carriage. At once the driver let out a furious hissin' sound, an' turnin' around, Joanna saw a dreadful, marvellous thing. The sheet beneath which lay the dead body of Great Uncle Tobacco was tremblin', tremblin' as with one last effort of will from beyond the grave. An' now, as Joanna watched, it fell away an' one stick-thin arm come out, an' one tremblin' hand emerged an' were raised up high an' then, as if it were costin' all the effort in the world, one tobacco-stained finger stretched out an' pointed, very clear an' very definite it pointed – to the path on the right. For a moment what seemed longer than time, it hung there, like

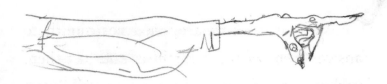

a beacon in the night – an' then it fell back, unmovin', an' never again did it stir.

Joanna seemed to feel a great mist clear from her mind as the music of that impossible city faded away on the wind.

'Driver,' she commanded, 'Take me home. Take me home to Lamonic Bibber.'

Mutterin' an' a-cursin', the driver took the reins once more an' they set off along the right-hand path. An' as they did so, Joanna couldn't resist one glance back at that city – but it weren't no place of wonders an' light no more, an' she quickly looked away again.

Within the hour she was warmin' herself in front of a roarin' fire what the maid had prepared, an' never more pleased to be back home. The driver had left without a word, only helpin' to get her old unc's body into the parlour an' then takin' off into the night, him an' his infernal carriage an' his team of breakneck horses – an' where they went next I do not know.

Joanna Vale buried her old uncs in the churchyard the followin' Sunday, an' though she missed him dearly, she knowed as he had led a long an' useful life an' she vowed to do the same herself. An' sure enough, she gone on to be a very successful lady indeed. Become a writer, so she did, one of the finest of her time, turnin' out gruesome novels where fiends an' ghoulies an' phantoms o' the night was always after innocent young men an' women – but where good always prospered in the end.

But though her stories was dark as dark can be, her life was filled with happiness an' smiles an' laughter. An' if anyone ever asked her what was the secret to her happiness, she would just look thoughtful for a moment an' say, 'I chose the right path in life.' An' if, in that moment, she was thinkin' about what she saw when she looked back at that city behind her – how it had changed an' what it had become – I dunno, an' what's more, I don't want to know. But then she'd smile again, an' it were as if the sun come back out on her face an' she were herself again.

Course, these days, there's many a road in an' out of Lamonic Bibber. An' that great tree what once stood where Joanna Vale saw the fork in the road has long been cut down, an' there's one of them Tesco's there now, what's quite handy one way an' another, although it do seem a shame in another way. But times change, so they do, yar, yar, so they do, yar.

Well now, if you didn't know it I've told it an' if you did know it I've told it anyhow. Sweet dreams, boys an' girls, sweet dreams.

THE END

Bibbering Through The Ages
Madame Strawberries

Madame Strawberries (1814–1878) was Lamonic Bibber's most successful strawberry-seller of all time. Born in Paris, Vienna, Algeria, Nowhere and Switzerland, she lived a carefree life until the age of six, when she was dropped into the English Channel by a raucous ostrich. For years she wandered the ocean bed, finally washing up on the

shores of Lamonic Bibber covered in seaweed and with a lobster hanging from her nose. By now Madame Strawberries had grown into an old woman and she soon became a familiar figure around town. Each summer she would wander the streets with her basket of strawberries and her nose-lobster, calling out in her pretty French accent: 'Buy some strawberries or I'll burn your house down.' Much loved by the local children, who would punch and kick her in the back whenever they could, Madame Strawberries eventually died of 'caterpillar of the lungs', an illness I just made up.

The Victorian Age

The Victorian Age was a time of marvels and very silly hats. It was an age when science ruled the waves, and extraordinary breakthroughs in medicine, chemistry, biology and silly hats were reported every thirty-five seconds. Seemingly overnight, tremendous factories sprung up in the cities and towns,

churning out goods like never before and pumping out millions of tonnes of lovely fresh soot into the atmosphere for everyone to enjoy. It was an era when everything and anything seemed possible, especially working for almost nothing in a freezing cold factory and being crushed to death in an industrial accident. And it was all down to the ingenuity of some very special men and women – the Victorian inventors.

There were all manner of inventors during the Victorian Age. One of the most famous was Tobias Brip, who came up with many of the things that we take for granted today, including postage stamps, Easter eggs and photography. Then there was Tobias Brip's mum and dad, who invented Tobias Brip; Tobias Brip's grandparents, who invented Tobias Brip's mum and dad; and Tobias Brip's next-door neighbour, Charlie, who invented living next door to Tobias Brip and coming round from time to time to borrow a plate.

Also around this time were **Thomas Edison**, who invented the light bulb; **Thomas Cheddarson**, who invented the somewhat less popular cheese bulb; **Pappa Gustav**, a

Tobias Brip relaxing with his mother in the countryside, two weeks before he invented photography

mysterious fellow from Sweden who invented Sweden; **Amelia K Hustings**, an American schoolteacher who invented middle initials; **the Wright Brothers**, who invented aeroplanes; **the Wright Sisters**, who also invented aeroplanes because girls can invent aeroplanes too, so shut up; **Cuthbert Luthbert**, who invented standing in a field shouting 'PUMPERNICKEL! PUMPERNICKEL! RAH RAH RAH!'; and **Isambard Kingdom Brunel**, who invented isambards.

But of all the many hundreds of inventors of the Victorian Age, none was more famous than **Cribbins**. Cribbins was so famous that if you went up to anyone in Victorian times and said, 'Hey, have you heard of Cribbins?' they would instantly reply, 'What on earth are you doing in my house? Get out or I'll call the police.'

Cribbins lived, as you may have guessed, in the little town of Lamonic Bibber, in a curious building high on Boaster's Hill. This building was known as Whistler's Folly, and it was there that Cribbins conducted his experiments: trying to attach a crab's head onto a monkey's body; trying to separate butterflies into butter and flies; and spending weeks on end cooped up in the observatory with his telescope, wondering how to use it.

Whatever he was up to – conducting experiments; inventing a device that first gently polished, and then completely pulverised, valuable antique furniture; or simply throwing a dishcloth at a rabbit for a joke – Cribbins was a wonder, and his work was known far and wide. Queen Victoria thought he was so brilliant that she named an entire country after him – Australia.

And yet, for all his fame, the later chapters of Cribbins' life have for years remained shrouded in mystery. No one seemed to know what became of him – until now. You see, recently an old diary came to light, written by Cribbins' closest friend, a certain Doctor Wempers. And within its pages lies a tale so *shocking*, a story so *astounding*, an account so downright *outrageous* that you will have to judge for yourself whether it is true or whether its author was simply an uncontrollable weirdo whose brains had gone all mucked up from too much beer and oysters. Whatever the facts of the matter, it is thanks to Doctor Wempers that we present . . .

1886

The

STRANGE CASE

of

DOCTOR WEMPERS

and

MR CRIBBINS

From the diary of Doctor Wempers

Thursday 11th November, 1886 - 12.30pm
Hello. I am Doctor Wempers, a remarkable Physician and Scholar who is a very good friend of that famous Scientist, Cribbins. Hmm, I wonder why I felt the need to introduce myself like that, after all, this is my private diary that I have been writing in for years and years, it seems a bit odd that I'd bother reminding myself who I am, oh well, never mind.

Today has been quite dull so far. I have spent the morning seeing patients; mixing ointments and tinctures; answering correspondence; buying a new top hat, monocle, pocket-watch, waistcoat and handkerchief; and generally being very Victorian indeed. Hmm, I am quite hungry. I might have beer and oysters for lunch.

Thursday 11th November, 1886 - 3pm
Had beer and oysters for lunch.

Thursday 11th November, 1886 - 11.40pm
Have just returned from the Lamonic Bibber Gentlemen's Club, where the strangest thing occurred! It was a cold night and Cribbins and I were sat in front of the fireplace, sampling a new spirit called brandy, which Cribbins himself had recently invented by taking a bottle of wine and crossing out the word 'WINE' and writing 'BRANDY' on the label instead.

Other than ourselves, the Club was almost empty. Only a few old duffers sat around in the deep leather armchairs, drowsing over their newspapers or sucking on their great-pipes and periodically coughing up disagreeable hunks of black phlegm onto the carpet.

Presently, Cribbins turned towards me, and he looked so grave that I thought to myself, 'he looks so grave.'

I studied my friend's face closely in the flickering firelight: the noble forehead, from which the dark hair receded severely; the elegant eyebrow, joined and all of one piece, as if someone had secretly done quite a thin and hairy poo above his eyes while he slept; the straight, proud nose; the high, fine-boned cheeks; the other things on his face I simply can't be bothered to go into, his chin, for instance. Cribbins' face was the face of a genius, that was for certain. But tonight it was the face of a troubled genius, I thought.

'Doctor Wempers,' said Cribbins. 'You and I have been friends for many years. Of all my acquaintances, you know more of my secrets than any. And yet there is one secret that lies so close

to my heart that I am afraid it shall grow and grow, strangling me from the inside like a horrible cauliflower, unless I let it out.'

'Come now,' said I, using a new invention called a 'mouth' that Cribbins had invented only that morning. 'Tell me what is on your mind.'

'Here is my dreadful secret,' lamented Cribbins. 'I . . . I am an utter failure.'

Now, this left me completely agog. I had been partially agog before in my life, of course, who hasn't – but never <u>completely</u> agog. It was quite painful, being that agog.

'You? A failure?' I spluttered, accidentally getting a bit of spit in Cribbins' hair, though he either did not notice or did not care. 'My dear Cribbins, you are nothing of the sort! You have discovered over three thousand new species of moustache! You have grown a new type of hazelnut that is slightly nicer than a normal hazelnut! You have devised a machine called a "Woosking Naffler" which is so ingenious that it does nothing at all! Why, you are no less than the greatest Scientist of this Age or any other! You are the furthest thing from a failure I could imagine!'

'No!' cried Cribbins, starting from his chair. 'It all means nothing! Nothing whatsoever! Unless I can achieve the "Ultimate Experiment", I will never be worth a copper penny!'

And so saying, he turned on his heel and ran out into the dark winter night without so much as stopping to tip good old Bleevens, the doorman.

I must say that the whole incident left me rather taken aback and I confess I ordered an extra-large helping of beer and oysters whilst I sat there mulling it over. Shortly thereafter, I returned home to my lodgings off the high street and here I sit now, writing my diary by lamplight. I wonder what has come over Cribbins, for I have never seen him like this before. And what did he mean by the 'Ultimate Experiment'? It all seems a great mystery to me!

Saturday 13th November, 1886
Nothing much has happened over the past forty-eight hours. I had beer and oysters for lunch yesterday and also today – but that is about all I have to relate.

Monday 15th November, 1886
Had beer and oysters for lunch. In the evening I took myself to see a performance of ''Tis Rubbish Being a Squirrel' at the Theatre Royale. Not one of old Terry's best, if you ask me (though I thought Henry Bancroft excellent as the shoe salesman).

Tuesday 16th November, 1886
Not a lot to report. Saw a street urchin outside the window. Had beer and oysters for lunch.

Wednesday 17th November, 1886
Guess what I had for lunch today? Beer and oysters.

Thursday 18th November, 1886
A curious day. I spent the morning waxing my moustache; putting my papers in order; throwing charitable tangerines and chestnuts out the window for the street urchins; steaming a plum pudding in my own hat; dressing up small dogs in ruffles; flying a sixty-foot-long airship around the living-room; feeding carrots and hay to my mad wife who lives in the attic; standing completely still for about three hours while Tobias Brip took

my photograph; boxing a kangaroo; and generally being even more Victorian than ever. I cannot remember what I had for lunch – oh, yes, it was beer and oysters.

In the evening I visited the Lamonic Bibber Gentlemen's Club, expecting to see Cribbins as usual, for the two of us have visited the Club together every Thursday evening for forty years or more. It has long been our custom to meet at eight o'clock prompt, and after a small supper of beer and oysters (although Cribbins himself never touches the oysters, he cannot stomach them), to repair to our comfy armchairs in front of the fireplace, there to sit in companionable conversation, talking over the issues of the day. This particular evening I was looking forward to seeing Cribbins more than ever, for I had not forgotten his strange behaviour of the previous *week and meant to challenge him on it. However, for the first time in forty years – Cribbins did not appear!*

'No Cribbins?' I said to myself. 'Surely he must be ill, although he seemed physically well enough when last we met. Still, the nights are growing cold and we are not so young as we used to be. Perhaps my dear friend has come down with the sniffles, or a bad case of the nits. But I am sure he will be in next week.'

Without Cribbins, the Club was not nearly so much fun, and I returned home far earlier than usual. Upon arriving back at my lodgings, I found a tremendously large wooden crate waiting for me at the top of the stairs. It contained dozens and dozens of bottles of Cribbins' recent invention, 'brandy'.

There was a note attached:

> I am sorry I couldn't make the Club
> tonight – but I shall see you soon.
> In the meantime, please accept this
> token of my apology.
>
> Your Friend,
> -C
> *xx*

Thursday 25th November, 1886

Once again there was no sign of Cribbins at the Club! I must confess I was not expecting this. I had been sure he would turn up tonight and had been looking forward to telling him how much I have been enjoying the brandy. It is a marvellous drink; I simply cannot get enough of it.

I cannot help but feel uneasy at my friend's continued absence. 'Surely he will turn up next week,' I told myself when I returned home, before pouring myself a little nightcap.

Thursday 2nd December, 1886

I can scarcely believe it but — no Cribbins! It is now three weeks running that he has not visited the Club. Perhaps I should pay my friend a visit. Yes. I am decided. I shall go to see him tomorrow, in that cursed laboratory of his.

Friday 3rd December, 1886

A day full of intrigue and curiosity. After an early lunch of brandy and oysters (I have discovered that brandy goes with oysters even better than beer!), I took myself off to Boaster's Hill, headed for Whistler's Folly. It was barely two o' the clock but already the light was fading from the sky. The snow fell thick and fast and the afternoon was bitterly cold.

'I wish I hadn't only worn a pair of pants and a vest,' I said to myself as, barefoot, I made my way up the hillside. 'What on earth was I thinking?'

Still, I persevered, for I was worried as to what had become of my friend; and also because I am a Victorian gentleman, and if there is one thing that Victorian gentlemen are good at, it is persevering. We are total persevere-ers.

Presently I reached my destination. Whistler's Folly is an odd sort of a place and I shall be honest – I have never much cared for it. There is something about those tall towers and the high iron railings that surround it, something forbidding, something almost . . . unnatural. As I rounded the final turn of the road, I thought that it had never looked so unwelcoming as it did at that moment, half-obscured by the flurries of snow and the thicket of conifers at its base. Suddenly I trembled to think of Cribbins, up there all alone with his beakers and his burners, and that phrase of his – the 'Ultimate Experiment' – came back to me, sending a chill through my entire body that had nothing to do with the weather.

'Hullo!' I called. 'Hullo, I say!'

I rapped twice on the great iron door but received no answer.

'Cribbins!' I cried. 'Let me in, for the love of God! It's freezing out here! I've been persevering all I can but I'm not sure that I can persevere much longer!'

Still there was no response, but suddenly, out of the corner of my eye (I was born with perfectly square eyes), I thought I detected movement. Yes, there! By the low wall that separated the main house from the observatory. Certainly I had discerned a flicker of – something. But what that something was, I could not say.

'Mysteriousness,' I muttered to myself. At once I left off at once from the front door and at once I at once hurried at once around the side of the building at once.

'Is anyone there?' I called. 'Show yourself or I'll – well, I don't know what I'll do, probably nothing, I'm not very good at fighting and I'm basically dressed in my underwear. But I say again, show yourself, you devil!'

Perhaps I spoke harshly, but I quite suspected I had discovered a thief, come to prey on Cribbins as he lay ill upstairs, or something of the sort. And indeed, when I reached the place where I had seen the movement, my worst fears seemed to be confirmed. There, amidst the thick drifts of snow and the dark green of the pines was – a face! A ghastly face, a frightful face! The face of a man, yes; but such a man as one would never wish to meet in one's dreams, let alone in waking life. The fearsome brow, the cruel eyes, the mean lips drawn back to reveal a perfectly hideous set of teeth, all crooked and rotten-looking, set in a grin not unlike that of Lucifer himself, I should fancy.

It gave me such a shock, coming upon it like that, that I gasped and clutched at my thinly-vested heart.

'Who – or _what_ – are you?' I managed. But the face merely continued to grin its horrible grin. And then I realised: it was no living thing, but rather some sort of exotic mask, hanging from one of the branches. As I watched, the mask turned *slowly in the breeze and a second face, previously hidden from sight on the reverse, came into view, this one of such fine and angelic proportions that it had the opposite effect of the first. My soul was lifted to see it – and, of course, there was the relief of having discovered not a criminal on Cribbins' property but merely an idle curiosity, perhaps something he'd brought back from one of his trips abroad as a younger man.*

But as the mask hung there, turning and turning in the wind, from angel to devil, from devil to angel, over and over, my misapprehensions returned in force. For some reason, the sight of the thing filled me with an unknowable, thrilling dread and I knelt there transfixed. The mask unsettled me – and yet I could not look away; until in due course there came a barking from a nearby dog or a demented infant, and abruptly I came to my senses.

'What!' I cried. Quite without my noticing, it had grown almost dark. With a start, I shook my head to clear it. Then I turned on my heel and fled, hurrying back down that hill as if all the devils of Hell were after me, for I wanted nothing but to get away from that place as fast as I could and to be back in my own lodgings.

By the time I reached my humble abode, I was rational again. The whole affair had shaken me, but surely that was nothing more than the effect of the falling snow and the growing darkness and the thirty-five glasses of brandy I had consumed before setting off. All the same, it had been an unnerving experience and my hand was not quite steady as I poured myself another drop. All else aside, today's trip was a failure: I still have not seen Cribbins. And such strange thoughts crowding in upon me . . . What to make of it all I do not know.

Sunday 5th December, 1886 - 10am

Oh what, oh what, oh what! I hardly know where to begin . . . It all seems like a terrible dream . . . But, alas, it is too, too real . . . Oh, what! Gracious! Oh, I must pull myself together. Perhaps some brandy and oysters will help settle my nerves . . . On second thoughts, I shall just take the brandy. For once in my life I seem to have no appetite for oysters.

Sunday 5th December, 1886 - Later

I am finally able to continue. What has thrown me is simply this: I have seen Cribbins at last! But rather than restoring my peace of mind his reappearance has left me full of questions and dark misgivings . . .

It all happened in the small hours of the morning. I had been asleep, dreaming of that queer mask as it turned from devil to angel, angel to devil, over and over. But then the faces grew confused. The mask turned again and I cried out in my dream, 'What! It is Cribbins! The face is Cribbins!'

Suddenly I found myself startled from my slumber by a sharp knock at the front door. Immediately I bounded from the bed, hurriedly pulling on my nightcap against the cold. I glanced at the grandfather clock in the hallway and saw that it was two in the morning.

'Who goes there?' I demanded. 'Knocking on people's doors at such an hour, what is this!'

Mustering all my courage I flung open the door – and there stood Cribbins upon the stair. Only what a change had come over the fellow in just a few weeks. For he looked so sallow and gaunt that I had immediately to hurry to the bookcase to look up what 'sallow' and 'gaunt' mean in the dictionary.

'Why, you seem like a man on the edge of death!' I remarked, and not untruly, for my friend was hardly recognisable. He had grown stick-thin and frail-looking. His clothes hung off him like great curtains. His eyes bulged wildly in their sockets as he stared desperately, almost madly, around my chambers. His hair had turned completely white and I noticed that he kept scratching and scratching his head as he talked. The scratching made me think that I had been right all along: Cribbins looked exactly like a fellow who was dying from a bad case of the nits.

'Doctor Wempers, my old friend,' croaked the ruined specimen before me. 'I am . . . There is no time to explain. I must . . . You must . . .'

But then he seemed to start, as if at some noise out on the street, although I myself had heard *nothing. With a tremulous hand, he removed a bottle of brandy from his waistcoat pocket and took a long swig before continuing.*

'I have written you a letter! Take it!' cried Cribbins so desperately that he scored a forty on the 'Desperate Cry-O-Meter' I always keep by my front door – one of the highest scores ever recorded.

'Take it! Take it!' he urged, thrusting a sealed envelope up my nostril and scratching at his head like a man possessed. 'It will explain everything! But you must never read it!'

'What's the point in you giving it to me then?' I asked.

'Well, on second thoughts you can read it, I suppose,' said Cribbins. 'But only in the event of my death. Until that time you must carry it around with you wherever you go, unopened, with all its secrets intact!'

'Do I have to carry it around like this?' I asked. 'Sticking out of my nostril?'

'Yes,' said Cribbins. 'For that is where I have placed it and that is where you must carry it at all times.'

'What about when I am in the bath?' I demanded. 'What then, Cribbins?'

'It is simple,' said Cribbins, swigging at his brandy once again. 'You must just keep your head above the water to protect the letter from getting wet. Now – there is no time, I must make haste!'

But I wasn't done yet for my keen mind had discovered a thing that I needed to say with my mouth because of the thoughts that my keen mind had made in my head.

'Hang on,' I implored. 'What if I go to the public baths for a swim? What then, Cribbins? You can hardly expect me to keep my head above water when I am going for a swim!'

'I hadn't thought of that,' admitted Cribbins. 'Hmm. OK. If you go for a swim you can take the letter out of your nose and put it somewhere safe. On a shelf, for instance. But the rest of the time you must keep that letter sticking out of your nose. It is vitally important!'

'Is it?' I asked. 'Is it really?'

'Yes,' said Cribbins. 'And – I nearly forgot – you must take this bag of fairy cakes and put it in your shoe. You must keep those fairy cakes in your shoe at all times! Yes, even when you go swimming, I'm afraid! It is vitally impo—'

But at this I drew the line. 'I am sorry, Cribbins,' I said. 'I am willing to constantly carry this letter around up my nose but this thing with the fairy cakes is too much.'

'OK, never mind about the fairy cakes,'

said Cribbins. 'To be honest, I was just trying to see if you'd fall for it, I thought it might be quite funny if you were always walking around with a bag of fairy cakes squishing about in your shoe. But the letter is vitally important, I assure you. Now – I must make haste! Remember,' he called over his shoulder as he took off down the stairs, still scratching at his head and swigging from his bottle, 'only open it in the event of my death!'

Wednesday 8th December, 1886
I spent the afternoon in Grosvenor Park with my old acquaintance, Splurchington, whom I had not seen for some months. We have been firm friends ever since we were at medical school together and we are very fond of each other. I don't want to kiss Splurchington or anything like that, I don't think. But I definitely like him. He has a friendly face and he always wears

a green hat, for as he likes to say, 'a green hat makes people think, "Ooh, look, that man's got green hair, oh, no, hang on, it's just his hat".'

Splurchington was in a fine humour and suggested that we hire a couple of penny-farthings and take them for a spin.

'But Splurchington,' I rejoined, 'you know very well that I am a terrible cyclist and have no sense of balance. I should end up in the rhododendrons with my be-trousered bottom wriggling in the air for all the world to see!'

Nonetheless, Splurchington persevered with his suggestion, for he is just as much a Victorian gentleman as I. In the end he was able to persuade me, and do you know what? I found that, from out of nowhere, I was the most excellent of cyclists! I sped through the park at a fantastic pace and took the corners with the greatest of ease. At one point

I even executed a perfect 'wheelie', which drew an admiring gasp from my companion.

'Goodness!' remarked Splurchington. 'Where on earth did you learn to ride like that?'

'I honestly don't know,' I said, as I rode around the duck pond like a man born to the job. 'It is a mystery to me, I'm sure.'

'Well, I've never seen anything like it,' replied Splurchington. 'Why, I wager that you'd even put Cribbins to shame – and he's the best penny-farthing rider I ever saw.'

'Ah, yes,' I said, all the gayness of the afternoon suddenly dropping away at the mention of our absent friend. By now we had reached the rose gardens, lonesome and without bloom at this time of year and I found myself plunged into the deepest melancholy.

'I have been thinking much about Cribbins,

Splurchington. I am worried about him.'

And with that, I related everything I knew of the case, beginning with Cribbins' running from the Gentlemen's Club; to the mask up at Whistler's Folly; to the unsettling visit of a few nights ago.

'Hmm,' said Splurchington, when the strange tale was done. 'Do you want to know what I think?'

But what Splurchington thought would forever go unsaid, for at that moment two old women happened by.

'Ooh, look,' said one of them, pointing at Splurchington. 'That man's got green hair, oh, no, hang on, it's just his hat.'

Splurchington burst into laughter at this, and somehow the moment passed and the subject of Cribbins was quite forgotten. At length I bid farewell to Splurchington, promising that we would meet up again before Christmas. Then I *came home. I thought that after all that exercise I should be as hungry as a racehorse but I had no real appetite and once again I passed up the opportunity for some oysters to go with my brandy. Not like me!*

Saturday 11th December, 1886
I have not written in my diary for a few days. Funny, but I hardly seem to be myself lately. Perhaps it is the worry, the endless worry of it all . . . And the not knowing. But certainly I have been right off my food. Yesterday I had brandy and oysters for lunch; but I had no sooner slurped up the first oyster than I spat it out in distaste.

'Yick!' I cried. 'Odious things!' For they seemed all too salty and slimy, and not to my liking at all.

'Cor blimey! Doctor Wempers off 'is oysters?'

remarked a street urchin called Jeff the Meff, who was walking by at that moment, whistling and juggling tangerines and chestnuts as he went. 'Wot ever next?' he said, sticking his grubby face through the open window. 'Queen Victoria playin' tiddlywinks against a Chinese pig?'

For it is well known that I love my oysters more than any man alive! Perhaps I am coming down with an illness, I should probably go and see a doctor, hang on, I _am_ a doctor, I should probably go and see myself, hang on, you can't really go and see yourself, can you? Can you? Oh, I don't know, I am tired and weak from hunger and so confused – confused by life; by oysters; by this whole business with Cribbins; by how Jeff the Meff could even have stuck his head through my window in the first place, seeing as I live on the fifth floor . . . It is all too confusing, too confusing by half!

Tuesday 14th December, 1886

I have spent the past few days in bed, nursing myself with brandy, hardly wanting to face the world and quite unable to stomach an oyster. In fact, if I even think about oysters I am automatically sick all over the place, so I'd better try not to think about oy—

BLLLLLEEEUUURRRRRRGGGGGH!

Even sleep affords me no comfort. If I so much as close my eyes I see nothing but that strange mask, the faces turning in the wind . . . Oh, it is awful.

Saturday 18th December, 1886

Too weak to write today. What will become of me?

Monday 20th December, 1886

I feel a little better today. Splurchington came to visit me in bed, I don't mean he got into bed with me, that would be fairly unacceptable, he just sat at my bedside and told me the news of the outside world.

'I'm worried about you, old chap,' said Splurchington. 'You don't seem yourself at all. Why, I hardly recognised you when I came in. In fact, if I hadn't known any better . . .'

But here he trailed off, his face white. Even his hat had turned white, don't ask me how but it was true.

'What is it?' I asked querulously.

'Listen,' said Splurchington very slowly, as if he were thinking things through very carefully indeed. 'I . . . I don't suppose you've been dining on your usual oysters lately, have you?'

'BLLLLLEEEEEUUUUURRRRRGGGH!' Hardly had Splurchington put the image in my head than I absolutely let go all over his face.

'Sorry, Splurchington,' I said. 'I'll have the maid come and lick your face clean immediately.'

'It matters not, it matters not!' said Splurchington, his strong features lost in thought and also lost in massive disgusting bits of sick so that he looked like a very unpleasant snowman, or just a kind of filthy 'Chunk Monster'.

'I have to make some enquiries,' said Splurchington. 'If what I think is happening is happening then something is happening that I did not expect to be happening but it is happening nonetheless. Doctor Wempers, you must rest. Try to conserve your strength, for we must pay a certain individual a visit on Christmas Eve.'

'You mean –' said I, trembling all over.

'Indeed,' said Splurchington, 'we must venture to Whistler's Folly. For there the truth will be found.'

Friday 24 December, 1886 - Christmas Eve

What a day this has been. What a day, and more, what an evening – the Eve of the birth of our Saviour, no less. It should have been a happy, even joyous, day – and yet instead it was a day of terrors and horrors and scares like something from the pages of a penny dreadful, or one of those Joanna Vale novels my wife was so fond of before she lost her wits!

'Well done, you made it out of bed,' said Splurchington when I met him at the bottom of Boaster's Hill.

'Indeed I did, though I hardly know how,' said I, sipping from the bottle of brandy I had brought along to give me strength. 'I have been so sick and feeble – and yet, curiosity and mystery got the better of me and I have roused myself and here I stand. And yet – do I? Do I stand here

at all? For what are we, Splurchington, what are any of us really, but reflections and spirits and memories and things like that? Are any of us real? Lately I seem to catch myself thinking that we are all merely phantoms, insubstantial things no more solid than the snowflakes which are falling around us as I speak.'

My mind was in a turmoil, as if I were underwater and disoriented and I hardly even knew what I meant by such words!

'I am . . . I . . . Sorry,' I gasped, leaning on my friend for support. 'I have been . . . I barely know what I am saying. I am not well, a great change is coming over me . . .'

But though I was raving like a lunatic, Splurchington merely nodded and muttered, 'Yes, yes. It is all coming clear. It is as I feared . . .'

Together we started up Boaster's Hill in the

fading light, Splurchington supporting me as I struggled feebly on. I thought of my last trip up here, which had ended so strangely. It seemed like a hundred years ago. On the lower slopes, a group of children stood in a half-circle, singing a traditional Christmas carol, their voices pure and lovely in the wintry haze.

'Look at those children, Splurchington,' I said as we ascended. 'They are so innocent. What do they know of the cares of the world? What understanding can they have of strange disappearances and frightening masks and knocks on the door in the middle of the night and all such bad lucks as I fear are gathering around us? None! And long may it remain, for childhood is a time of frolic and play, a special time, a blessed time – yes, most especially so during this hallowed season in which our Lord and Saviour

was delivered unto the world that He might take the sum weight of human folly and sin upon His own broad shoulders in order to alleviate the burden of Mankind – oh, long may those childhood days stretch out unencumbered by the wearying cares of the adult world, for in the innocence of the young we see ourselves not only as we once were, but also as we hope one day to be again, one day in that life beyond this, one everlasting day in the shining glory of Heaven, when all worries and woes shall fall away from us and we are born anew to bask in the golden light of our Creator; and on that day the trumpets shall sound and in our Deliverance we shall once again know the pure and good, we shall at last attain our Eternal Reward. In the innocence of the young we see it all, Splurchington – what has been; and what is; and what shall come to be; and oh, it gives me hope, my friend, it gives me hope indeed!'

'What was that?' said Splurchington, 'I wasn't really listening.'

'Oh, nothing,' I replied. And together we continued on in silence.

~ ~ ~

Presently we came upon Whistler's Folly, where, we hoped, the answer to the conundrum would be found. Once more I was struck by the dismal aspect of the place. The stone walls seemed sterner and more intimidating than ever, the tall towers glowered down upon us, the high iron railings were friend to no man . . . Splurchington, however, appeared undaunted and, marching briskly to the front door, he rapped smartly upon the brass knocker that hung there and which was fashioned into the shape of a lion's head.

'Cribbins!' shouted Splurchington. 'It is I – Splurchington!'

'And it is I – Doctor Wempers!' I shouted.

'And it is I – Ploopy!' shouted Splurchington in a different voice, a sort of nasal squeal.

'What was that about?' I enquired of my companion.

'Oh, it was just an idea,' said Splurchington in embarrassment. 'I suddenly thought, "What if Cribbins has got a really good friend called 'Ploopy' and he hasn't seen Ploopy in ages and even though he won't open up for _us_, if he thinks that Ploopy's outside he might at least open up for _him_?" I know, I know, it was a silly idea, I see that now.'

Ploopy or no Ploopy, there was no answer from the resident of Whistler's Folly – but, glancing up, I thought I saw a shadowy figure appear momentarily at the very top of the East tower, before suddenly ducking from view!

'Excitements!' I said.

'I knew it . . . It all fits!' cried Splurchington, and he began throwing himself violently against the wooden frame of the door. Again and again he smashed himself against the entrance until suddenly the old latch gave and the door flew open!

'Good God!' I shouted. 'What has been going on in here?'

The entire building was in disarray. Test tubes, beakers, flasks bubbling over with noxious-smelling chemicals – all lay strewn in heaped confusion on the worktops. Broken glass and screwed-up balls of paper covered with the crazy scribblings of a madman littered the filthy floor and the walls were daubed with yet more scribbles and filth.

'Good God!' I shouted again. 'What has he been up to?'

For it was now all too clear that Cribbins had crossed the line from respectable genius to utter lunatic. In front of our very eyes, a cat whose brain had been swapped with that of a dog barked and chased itself around the room. In the far corner sat a gigantic Frankenstein with a metal head, but luckily it was on recharge, so it wouldn't be able to get us for a few hours yet. As we stood there, mouths agape, a monkey with the head of a crab leapt from the ceiling and went racing out into the night. But there were other horrors besides, and we had no choice but to fight our way through them all. There was a donkey who could teleport, he was really hard to get rid of, but eventually Splurchington got him by just standing in one place and kicking at the air over *and over until the donkey accidentally teleported into where Splurchington's foot was and fell over dead. There was a child's doll that had been wired up to a piano and could fire musical notes out of its eyes. There was a leopard, who wasn't a monster or anything – but it was still a leopard, which is bad enough. And more, so very many more . . . One by one we fought off the unnatural fiends until we reached the bottom of the spiral staircase that led to the East tower.*

'Get lost, cheesy!' cried Splurchington, kicking a giant mouse out of the way – and with that, my fearless companion began racing up the stone steps, taking them two and three at a time. I followed him by basically looking at what he was doing and then doing the same sort of thing but just a little bit after him. As I rounded the final flight, I heard a confusion of raised voices and the

sounds of a considerable tussle. Sick with fear and foreboding, I burst into the small round chamber at the top of the tower to discover Splurchington kneeling over a cloaked figure that lay sprawled upon the floor.

'Come on, come on, man!' Splurchington was yelling. 'Come on!'

Desperately he pressed down on the cloaked figure's chest, attempting to revive it somehow, or maybe just because he enjoyed desperately pressing down on people's chests in macabre towers, perhaps I will never know. Again and again Splurchington pressed down, but it was all in vain.

'It is no good,' Splurchington said, wiping the sweat from his brow. 'He is gone.'

In the distance the church bells chimed, calling the faithful to Midnight Mass on this most unusual of Christmas Eves. I sat myself down on a stool beneath the narrow window and tried to make sense of it all.

'Cribbins dead,' I muttered. 'I can hardly believe it. Cribbins dead, and no explanation of – hang on! The letter!'

'?' said Splurchington, who was so exhausted that he couldn't even say any words, he could only do a question mark.

'Cribbins gave me a letter, look!' I exclaimed. 'He stuck it up my nose, I have been carrying it with me all along! He instructed me only to read it in the event of his death! Well, now he _is_ dead! Here, Splurchington!' I cried, ripping it from the envelope. 'Read it, read it, do!'

'I'm not touching that,' said Splurchington in disgust. 'It's just spent two weeks up your hooter.'

And so, with trembling hands, I myself

unfolded the yellowing paper and began reading it aloud – and slowly the last pieces of the mystery fell into place.

CRIBBINS' LETTER

Saturday 4th December, 1886

Dear Doctor Wempers,

Hello. If you are reading this then it means that I am dead. And yet, I think if you continue to read, you will discover that there is a riddle in that first line; for I am not dead at all. How is that? I shall explain in good time. But first I must tell you something.

Doctor Wempers, I hate you. I have always hated you. You are an idiot. Always writing in your stupid diary about what you had for lunch. And you call yourself a doctor but I have never seen you do anything useful for anyone. I don't even like those gloves you wear on cold days, they are stupid gloves, I don't know if anyone's ever told you but they're just – I hate them. They're stupid gloves.

Now, Doctor Wempers (or as I secretly enjoy calling you, 'Doctor Durr-Brain') you might be saying to yourself, 'Why, if Cribbins hated me so much, did he put up with my friendship for so long? Why did he continue to accompany me to the Lamonic Bibber Gentlemen's Club every Thursday for over forty years, discussing matters of Science and Medicine and such?' Well, it is a good question and one which deserves an answer.

Many years ago, when I was a much younger

man, I happened to travel to the South Sea Islands. There I saw many peculiar sights and learnt many strange things about the Nature of Life – how to catch lobsters using an old sock; how to do that thing where you throw a pebble into the sea and it goes 'bouncy bouncy bouncy bouncy bouncy' on the water; how perhaps we can control our Destinies by using the evils of Science to swap our identities with those of other people; all sorts of things.

I brought back an interesting two-faced mask from my travels – perhaps you have seen it? It is a mere curiosity; but strangely fascinating. I often found myself gazing at it for hours on end as it turned in the breeze, one face seeming to become another, and it was this that gave me my grandest idea of all: how to swap my own face with that of another. And not only the face, but the whole body and mind and spirit too – in short, how to transfer my life to another human being! And thus the 'Ultimate Experiment' was born.

But the undertaking required one thing above all others – a human subject. I cast my eye far and wide to find someone to experiment on and eventually, Doctor Wempers, I bumped into you at the Club, all those many years ago.

'Hello,' I said to myself. 'This upstart of a doctor seems like just the fool! I shall carefully pretend to be his friend for the next forty years and then, just when he is not expecting it, the Experiment shall begin.' And so you see, all this time, I have been laying my plans.

As the years passed, I did indeed become the greatest inventor of this Age or any other. But even as the world marvelled at my inventions, I was secretly working on the Ultimate Experiment, perfecting the chemistry that would bring me my greatest reward.

Towards the end of summer this year, I became suddenly ill. I caught a bad case of the nits and knew that my time on this Earth was short. There was nothing for it – I had to hurry the rest of my work. Do you remember that new drink I invented a few weeks ago? 'Brandy'? Well, that was not just a lovely drink that makes you giggle and say embarrassing things and fall down in the gutter after all! No, it was my Secret Formula! It was the beginning of the Ultimate Experiment! The more you drank of my 'brandy', Doctor Wempers, the more my dark Science was doing its work.

Have you noticed, over the past few weeks, that you have not exactly been 'feeling yourself'? Do you remember how you used to love eating oysters but now you can't even think of them without being sick? Do you recall how I, Cribbins, cannot stand oysters? It makes me sick even to think of – BLLLLEEEEEUUURRRRRRRRGGGGGH! My apologies, do excuse me.

Doctor Wempers, have you, by any chance, happened to try cycling a penny-farthing lately? Did you find that even though you used to be one of the most rubbish cyclists the world has ever known, you were now suddenly magnificent at it? Do you recall how I, Cribbins, have always been a tremendous cyclist and have won all sorts of shiny cups and medals and kisses from pretty ladies by taking part in penny-farthing-riding competitions?

Well, put it all together, man, if you have

not already. You see, over the past few weeks, YOU have been turning into ME. And I have been locked up in this chamber, slowly dying of the nits but craftily turning into YOU at the same time, so that I should not die after all. For in swapping our places, I have also cured myself of the nits and given them to you and you shall die of them instead of me, sorry about that.

Merry Christmas, Cribbins!

Love from
Cribbins
xx

~ ~ ~

'Then it is all true,' said Splurchington, once the letter was through. He was looking at me

very strangely. 'I saw it, oh, I saw the change in you, but I didn't want to believe it! But let us be absolutely sure.'

The cloaked figure still lay upon the floor, one ghastly hand flopped across its face. Gently, Splurchington moved the hand aside. Slowly he pulled back the hood.

And there before us was Doctor Wempers, dead as the day he was born.

He was unmoving, now and forevermore, the only signs of life the thousands of nits scuttling heartlessly through his hair. Those nits had once belonged to me, I realised – but now I was free.

'The change is final then,' I said in triumph – for now I was fully myself and I dared to speak my own name at last! 'I, Cribbins, live again!'

A small mirror hung askew by the window and it was to this that I now directed my attention. And *gazing into the dusty glass, I saw the final proof.*

It was all there. The noble forehead, from which the dark hair receded severely; the elegant eyebrow, joined and all of one piece, as if someone had secretly done quite a thin and hairy poo above my eyes while I slept; the straight, proud nose; the high, fine-boned cheeks; the other things on my face I simply can't be bothered to go into, my chin, for instance.

I had the face of a genius. An evil genius.

'The Ultimate Experiment was a total success, as I always knew it would be!' I cried in my new, extremely Cribbins-y voice. But then I noticed something. Some nits were running around in my hair. They must have jumped onto my head while I had been examining Doctor Wempers' corpse a moment before!

'Curses,' I muttered under my breath, which

is the very best place to mutter. 'It has begun again.'

'Whatever is the matter, Cribbins?' cried Splurchington, who was struggling to take it all in.

'Oh, nothing, nothing,' I replied. Turning away from my companion I carefully removed the bottle of brandy from my pocket. Then I crossed out the word 'BRANDY' and wrote 'GIN' on the label instead.

'Splurchington, my dear chap,' I said, laying a friendly hand upon his shoulder. 'It has been a most extraordinary day and we have been through much together. Would you care to try a brand new drink I have just invented?'

THE END

Bibbering Through The Ages
CHIMPY ROBERTS

Chimpy Roberts was Lamonic Bibber's first ever dustman. He was born in New South Poland in 1911 and died in 1851, which makes him the only man in history to have died before he was born. In 1890 he moved to Lamonic  Bibber to escape from a man with a frightening hand. Chimpy Roberts had thirty children but he couldn't be bothered remembering their names, so he just called them all 'Elizabeth', even though they were all boys. Although he was a dustman, Chimpy Roberts never once emptied out anyone's bins. Instead he just sat at home all day long, playing with a very nice gooseberry.

1916

To My Wife, Mary

-- -- -- -- -- -- -- -- -- -- --
Written by Private Curly Henderson
of the Lamonic Biber
2nd ~~IXXX~~ Infantry Brigade.
-- -- -- -- -- -- -- -- -- -- --

DOOF.

That is the sound of the War, all
around.

DOOF.

Enemy soldiers firing artillery at
us.

DOOF.

Oh, for goodness' sake. They just
fired another one.

DOOF.

Don't they ever sleep? All they do
all day is just -
DOOF. DOOF.

They just did two of them.
DOOF. DOOF. DOOF. DOOF. DOOF.

I honestly can't believe how
wasteful they're being with their
artillery shells.
DOOF.

Oh no, that one got my mate,
Ginger, in the leg!
DOOF.

Ginger! Are you all right?
DOOF.

Ginger! Ginger! Talk to me, Ginger!
DOOF.

Ginger just died, it's a disgrace.
DOOF.

That was one of ours, we're firing
back at them now. Serves them
right.

DOOF.

Take that, you lot! For England!
And for Ginger!

DOOF.

That was one of theirs again, I
thought they'd run out but no, it
turns out they've still got loads
of ammunition left. Typical.

DOOF. DOOF.

That was one of ours, followed by
one of theirs.

DOOF.

I don't even know who let that one
off, this is a nightmare.

DOOF.

I really hate the War.

DOOF.

You never have a moment's peace.

DOOF.

I think if you asked me, 'What
do you prefer, Curly? Lying in a
muddy ditch while the enemy fires
huge exploding artillery shells at
you or sitting at home in front
of the fire, doing the crossword
while having a drop of ale and
cuddling your lovely wife?' I'd
probably go for the second choice.

DOOF.

Oh my God! You know how a minute ago
I said Ginger died? It turns out he
was only pretending! What a joker he
is! This is the best day ever!

338

DOOF.

> Oh, COME ON. Another one just got
> Ginger in the face and now he's
> really dead after all. This is the
> worst day ever.

RAT-A-TAT-A-TAT!

> Great. Now they're running at us
> and firing machine guns. And it's
> raining. And my feet hurt. And the
> food's terrible. Last night they
> gave us a plate of what they said
> was beef stew, well it didn't taste
> like beef to me, I'll tell you that
> for nothing. And there was something
> that looked suspiciously like a tail
> floating around in the gravy.

DOOF. RAT-A-TAT! BOOM! BOOM! RAT-A-
TAT-A!

This is a complete nightmare. I
wish I were back home with you,
Mary, my love.

DOOF. DOOF.

That is the sound of my heart,
Mary.

DOOF. DOOF. DOOF.

My heart beating for you.

DOOF.

Despite the mud and the blood and
the rats and the fear.

DOOF.

And Ginger's exploded head.

DOOF. DOOF. DOOF. DOOF. DOOF.

I know in my heart I shall see you
again.

DOOF.

My heart will never stop beating

for you, Mary.

DOOF. DOOF.

As long as I live I shall always

RAT-A-TAT-A-TAT-A-TAT-A!

I shall always, with every beat of
my heart

DOOF. RAT-A-TAT-A-TAT-A-TAT-A-! DOOF.

DOOF.

I shall always

DOOF.

I shall always lov

Bibbering Through The Ages

FRANK NERBLES

Born on a roller coaster in 1928, Frank Nerbles was an unpleasant baby who grew into a pointless layabout of a man. In 1962, after years of smoking, gambling and drunkenly fighting chickens, he suddenly announced that he was going to beat the Americans into space and become the first man to walk on the moon. No one took him seriously, but Frank kept at it and on July 20, 1969, about half an hour before Neil Armstrong showed up, he finally achieved his dream. An estimated six people worldwide tuned in to watch on TV as Frank Nerbles stepped from the rocket he'd cobbled together out of a couple of milk crates and some fireworks, and uttered his immortal words: 'It's rubbish up here. No pubs, no betting shops, no nothing. Just a load of sports equipment.' Upon his return to Earth, he was welcomed as a hero until it was discovered that he hadn't been to the moon at all, he'd broken into a gym after twelve pints of cider and become slightly confused.

1974

Brian Six

*O*nce upon a time, two or three miles to the north of Lamonic Bibber, there lived a boy who stood four feet tall and who weighed five stone. His name was Brian Six and he was seven years old and he lived at number 8,

Nine Lane, in the town of Ten. This story starts at eleven o'clock with Brian and twelve of his friends – that makes thirteen people in all.

It was a grey, rainy April 14th and Brian and his friends took the number 15 bus to go and see a film called *Sixteen*. It was the seventeenth time they had tried to see this film, but when they got to the cinema the man wouldn't let them in.

'I'm sorry, you have to be eighteen or over to see this film,' said the man. 'I can see it because I'm nineteen. And I've seen it twenty times already and it's brilliant.'

So Brian said goodbye to his friends and went home, taking the number 21 bus this time. But halfway home it broke down and he had to take the number 22 bus instead. But soon that bus broke down as well and he had to wait twenty-three minutes in the pouring rain, watching as twenty-four cars drove by before a taxi appeared and took him the rest of the way home.

'That'll be twenty-five pounds, please,' said the taxi driver.

'There's twenty-six,' said Brian, who knew you should always give a tip. 'Always give a tip' was the twenty-seventh item of good advice on his dad's 'LIST OF TWENTY-EIGHT PIECES OF GOOD ADVICE', which he always read out to Brian on Brian's birthday – the 29th of September.

Thirty minutes later, Brian was doing his maths homework. Question thirty-one was 'what is 32 + 33?' and question thirty-four was 'what is 35 x 36?'

Brian didn't have a clue so he just put '37' and '38' and moved on to his English homework, an essay entitled 'Thirty-Nine Things I'd Like

To Do Before I'm Forty'. After that he did his geography homework, which was to list forty-one different countries in Africa.

The next day when Brian handed in his homework, he found out he'd done really badly. He'd only got 42% for his maths homework, 43% for his English homework and 44% for his geography homework.

'I'm very disappointed in you,' said his maths teacher, Mr Fortyfive.

'I'm disappointed in you as well,' said his English teacher, Mrs Fortysix.

'Me too,' said his geography teacher, Mr Ibetyouthoughtthissurnamewouldbeanother-numberbutitisnt.

After school, Brian ran home as fast as he could. He was just in time for his favourite TV show. It was called *Precinct 47* and it was about forty-eight policemen battling forty-nine robbers who had each stolen fifty pounds from fifty-one banks. The programme lasted fifty-two minutes and it was on Channel 53. Brian was especially excited because this week it was the fifty-fourth episode and *Fifty-Five* magazine had given it fifty-six stars out of fifty-seven, which was the highest rating they'd ever given a TV show in all their fifty-eight-year history. Fifty-nine of Brian's friends came round to watch it with him – that made sixty watching in all, or sixty-one if you counted Brian's dog, Sixtytwo. And they all agreed that it was sixty-three times better than the sixty-fourth episode of *Precinct 65*, which was a different TV show about sixty-six policemen battling sixty-seven robbers who had each stolen sixty-eight pounds from sixty-nine banks.

After the show was over, Brian's friends

went home.

'What shall I do now?' said Brian to himself seventy times.

'I'm bored,' he added, seventy-one times.

Just then he heard the sound of seventy-two trombones, and looking out of his window he saw seventy-three musicians parading down the street, each playing a trombone (except for the last guy in line, who had forgotten his).

Brian ran outside at seventy-four miles per hour and joined the parade, becoming the seventy-fifth musician in the band (another guy had joined just before Brian). They started playing a song called 'Seventy-Six Trombones', and they marched for seventy-seven miles. Eventually they reached the sea, where Brian got caught up amongst a group of tourists (there were seventy-eight of them, if I remember correctly) and in all the confusion, he accidentally ended up on a cruise liner called *The Seventy-Nine Smiles of King Neptune's Eighty Daughters*. The ship set to sea and Brian sobbed eighty-one tears to think that he'd never see any of his eighty-two friends again (he had some other friends I haven't told you about).

After eighty-three days, *The Eighty-Four Smiles of King Neptune's Eighty-Five Daughters* (the captain had changed the name of the ship halfway through the voyage) reached New York. Brian jumped ashore, ran down eighty-six steps into the subway and rode the number 87 train downtown to the corner of Eighty-Eighth Street and Eighty-Ninth Avenue, where he moved into apartment 90 of the Ninety-One Club, a famous establishment run by a ninety-two-year-old artist called Michael.

Brian spent
the rest of his
days there and
became a
famous artist
himself.
He painted
ninety-three pictures over
the years and he was just starting work on the
ninety-fourth when ninety-five pigeons flew
into his apartment, grabbed him and flew him
outside. They dropped him ninety-six feet to
the ground and he broke ninety-seven bones
in his body. Ninety-eight ambulances rushed
to the scene but they couldn't save him.

Brian died at the age of ninety-nine. And
do you know how many people came to his
funeral?

Eleven.

The End

THE FRUIT SCIENTISTS, THE TALKING GRAPES, THE CROWS OF THE FUTURE, THE DISCONNECTED-FACE-BUM-DOGS, THE PENCIL PEOPLE, THE NORMAL PEOPLE, THE ELECTRONIC NOIMPS, THE STUPID ANTS WITH HUMAN HANDS, THE UNITED STATES OF BEING A LION, THE SUBTERRANEAN KINGDOM OF THE CANNIBAL SKELETON ROBOTS, THE NON-EXISTENT MARTIANS, CHARLOTTE GLASS, THE HEXAGONAL PONY, THE GIANT WALKING CHESSMEN, THE CRUMBS OF THE SOUTH AND PLOVER

The whole thing started when a team of six Fruit Scientists from the International Lord Famous Research Institute of Lamonic Bibber began experimenting on grapes. They were trying to come up with an atomic grape, the tastiest and most powerful weapon of all time. But you know what Fruit Scientists are like – always bunking off to muck about with the watermelons or seeing who can flush the most oranges down the toilet in two minutes. What with all their larking about, they got a few of the calculations wrong and instead of atomic grapes, they were left with grapes that had funny little violet eyes and could talk.

At first the scientists thought this was hilarious (they even started trying to impress people they fancied at parties by pretending they'd meant to invent the Talking Grapes all along), but they soon came to regret what they'd done because the Talking Grapes were so annoying. They were so small that their voices were really high-pitched and squeaky, and eventually it got so irritating that the scientists decided to eat them just to shut them up.

However, this wasn't so easy. By now there were fourteen million Talking Grapes in the laboratory and there were only six Fruit Scientists (also, one of the scientists was allergic to grapes in the first place, so she was reluctant to eat her share). After a while the scientists got bored of eating the Talking Grapes and threw them in the bin.

But that's the trouble with science. Once you've created something like Talking Grapes, who knows where it will lead? While the scientists were busy working on their next experiment (trying to teach blueberries to play cricket) the bin outside the laboratory was being picked over by two of the most notorious scavengers of those times: the Disconnected-Face-Bum-Dogs[1] and the Crows of the Future.[2] After the Disconnected-Face-Bum-Dogs and the Crows of the Future had had their fill, wouldn't you know it, along came a large group of Pencil People[3] who quite fancied

1 The Disconnected-Face-Bum-Dogs were really weird. They were just a dog's face and no body and then, about half a mile away, a dog's bum. Nothing in between. What they'd do, right, the dog's face would go rolling along the ground hunting for snacks and when it came across something tasty, it would snaffle it up, and then a couple of hours later, half a mile away, the dog's bum, which was also rolling along, would suddenly come to a complete halt and do something unpleasant on the pavement. No one knew exactly how the Disconnected-Face-Bum-Dogs had come into being but the best guess was that it had something to do with the nuclear explosion that had taken place at the Barky-Barky Woof-Woof dog food factory in the 6030th century.

2 The Crows of the Future were just the same as normal crows, but in the future.

3 There were loads and loads of Pencil People in the future, far more than we have today. As you know, Pencil People look exactly the same as Normal People except they don't have heads, instead they just have thousands and thousands of pencils growing out of their necks. The Pencil People generally got on well with

a few Talking Grapes for lunch too. And just as the Pencil People were finishing up, some Normal People came along and polished off the last few stragglers that were rolling around at the bottom of the bin. Nearly

the Normal People except occasionally when some Normal Person might think, 'Oh, I came out without a pencil and I need to write something down, what shall I do? Oh, there's one of those pencil guys, that's convenient,' and they'd snap off one of the Pencil Person's pencils and then the Pencil Person would get annoyed and say something like, 'That's *so* disrespectful, you can't just go around snapping bits of my head off like that, I mean, seriously, that's *so* disrespectful.' Sometimes it would lead to a fight, but usually an Electronic Noimp[3a] would cruise over and calm everyone down before things could really get out of hand.

3a The Electronic Noimps were the police of the future. They were kind of just these large metal cubes that could fly and make decisions. They were originally invented by the ants. [3b]

fourteen million Talking Grapes lost their lives that day. It was one of the worst fruit massacres in history.

But why do I say *nearly* fourteen million? Why not all of them? Well, you see, there was one Talking Grape that didn't get eaten – and that grape's name was Plover. Plover was the smallest grape of the lot, so small that everyone had overlooked him in their frenzied quest to eat grapes. Later that evening, long

3b The ants had become super-intelligent around the middle of the 833rd century. The ants had always been *fairly* clever, but after a meteorite crashed into the Earth they became even more intelligent than people. Also around that time, they accidentally grew hands. The hands were really cool because they weren't ant hands, they were human hands, exactly the same size and shape as your hands or mine, but attached to ants. The hands made it a lot easier for the ants to build things, and together with their new super-intelligence they built the Electronic Noimps, just to see if they could. After they'd built the Electronic Noimps, the ants didn't really know what to do with them so they just let them loose in the streets and told them to be police officers. Shortly afterwards, another meteorite hit the Earth and turned all the super-intelligent ants into unbelievably stupid ants.[3c] So not only was the future full of Normal People, Pencil People, Fruit Scientists, Crows of the Future, Disconnected-Face-Bum-Dogs and Electronic Noimps – there were also millions of Stupid Ants with Human Hands waddling about everywhere, bumping into each other and saying things like, 'DER, I DON'T UNDERSTAND THINGS NO GOOD.'

after everyone had abandoned their horrifying meal, the bin toppled over and Plover rolled out onto the pavement, the last surviving member of his species, all alone in a cold, cold world.

'Today I have seen nature at its worst,' he squealed. 'Today I have witnessed thousands upon thousands of my grape brothers and sisters and cousins and aunties and nephews – all savagely chewed to bits by all manner of people and scientists and beasts! Why is there so much suffering in the world? Why can't everyone just get along?'

While Plover was lying there wondering what to do next, the Fruit Scientists came out of the building. They'd finished work for the day

3c At precisely the same time as the super-intelligent ants became stupid, the lions became super-intelligent, although it had nothing to do with the meteorite, it was just evolution. They immediately built a rocket with a mane on it and flew to Mars, where they started a new country called the United States of Being a Lion and they lived there for the rest of their days because they just preferred it up there because they thought it was fun because they liked it.

and were off down the holographic pub for a virtual shandy.

'What's this?' cried the head Fruit Scientist. 'I thought we'd got rid of all those grapes!'

'Looks like we missed one, boss,' said another, snatching up Plover and dangling him in the air. 'Not much of a specimen – but we can't let him live. He's just too squeaky.'

'Please don't eat me,' squeaked Plover. 'There is too much pain and suffering in the world! Why can't we all just get along?'

'Shut it!' sneered the scientist, but as he lifted Plover towards his mouth, Plover's thin green skin burst on the man's fingernail and a jet of delicious grape juice shot out and got him right in the eye.

'I'm blind! I'm blind!' cried the scientist, who was a bit of a cry-baby.

His hands flew to his face and Plover
went soaring through the air.

'I never meant to hurt anyone!' squealed Plover. 'Why can't we all just get along?'

'Stop that grape!' demanded the head Fruit Scientist, but Plover had tumbled into the gutter and before he knew it, he was caught up by a gust of wind and whisked away down the nearest drain. He was free!

» » »

But Plover's real troubles were only beginning. The drains were no place for a Talking Grape. They were damp and dark and dire, without a single ray of sunlight or of hope. No one knows how

Plover managed to stay alive down there for as long as he did. Perhaps he had to eat rats. Maybe he found a discarded sandwich. In any case, the scientists were furious that the last of their grapes had escaped. They began taking time off work to go down the drains, hunting Plover through the murk like a wild animal, powerful flashlights searching every nook and cranny, professional grape-rifles at the ready.

'We're going to get you! You've got no chance, Plover!'

The cruel words echoed along the tunnels, making Plover tremble – and yet somehow the little grape always managed to stay one step ahead. He was cunning and laid traps, and eventually, after months and months of pursuit, all six of the Fruit Scientists ended up

chained to the wall of his secret
underground lair.

'Please! Let us go!' they begged.

But Plover had absolutely no
idea how to let them go, as he
didn't have any hands or feet, and
in fact he sometimes wondered
how he'd even managed to trap the scientists
and chain them up in the first place.

'I'm sorry,' squeaked Plover. 'Why can't we
all just get along? I only want peace.'

A sudden rush of sewage swallowed him
up and he was whisked away down the tunnel
on the smelly brown tide. The Fruit Scientists
watched him disappearing into the distance,
getting smaller and smaller as he went. It didn't
take long, because he was already extremely
small to begin with.

'Well, that's that,' sighed the head Fruit Scientist. 'We're done for. We should never have meddled with those grapes.'[4]

» » »

The next twenty years were a nightmare for Plover. Tossed and turned on the frothing tides, spirited through the pitch-black tunnels, fighting off rats and other pests, narrowly avoiding the grinding jaws of the monstrous underground machines that ground relentlessly on and on beneath the Earth . . . On more than one occasion he came close to giving up altogether – but finally he managed to get out

4 Eventually the Fruit Scientists rotted away and became skeletons and then, because it was so damp and wet in the drains, they started to rust, so they became skeleton robots, and then they finally managed to break through their chains and start breeding and then they started eating each other to survive, even though if you eat each other to survive, quite a few of you don't end up surviving much at all. And that is how the vast Subterranean Kingdom of the Cannibal Skeleton Robots came into being, which was one of the rowdiest and most disgusting kingdoms of all time.

by jumping on a ledge.

'I wish I'd thought of that earlier,' squeaked Plover, squinting against the bright sunlight that he hadn't glimpsed in over two decades. 'Oh well, never mind. Here I am, back at last. And perhaps while I have been gone everyone has learnt to get along. Perhaps the world is finally at peace.'

But nothing could have been further from the truth. As Plover's eyes grew accustomed to the light, he realised that the world was now one huge battleground. And there he was, caught in the middle of it all. What had happened? How had it all come about? Well, it's a bit of a long story, so we'd better have another footnote.[5]

5   During the time that Plover had spent down the drains, the world had gone from bad to worse. The Disconnected-Face-Bum-Dogs had eaten so many Talking Grapes that their numbers had multiplied dramatically and there were now thousands and thousands of little doggy faces and little doggy bums by every lamp post, on every lawn, in every playground, in every park, in every house and school and building, all of them barking or eating or pooing like it

'It's madness!' cried Plover, once he'd read the footnote and brought himself up to date on current events. 'Utter madness!'

Seizing his chance, he jumped up and hid in the eye of a Hexagonal Pony[6] who happened to be passing by. As soon as the Hexagonal Pony was back home in the forest, Plover jumped out from its eye and told the Giant Walking Chessmen and the Crumbs of the South what

was the end of the world. You could hardly move for a Disconnected-Face-Bum-Dog's face in your Shreddies, or a Disconnected-Face-Bum-Dog's bum staring at you while you were in the shower. Eventually the Normal People decided the only thing for it was to wipe out the Disconnected-Face-Bum-Dogs by poking them in the snout using pencils, which they (the Normal People) snapped off the Pencil People's heads without even asking first. Obviously, that had caused the Pencil People to declare war on the Normal People *and* the Disconnected-Face-Bum-Dogs. And then, not wanting to feel left out, the Crows of the Future had declared war on *everyone*. With so much fighting everywhere, the Electronic Noimps had started malfunctioning and flying out of control. One of them had crashed into a drain covering, releasing thousands of the Cannibal Skeleton Robots into the streets. Of course, because they had once been scientists, the robots were excellent at computers and they quickly set to work reprogramming the Noimps to attack everyone else, even the Stupid Ants with Human Hands, who didn't understand what was going on and were panicking and punching everyone in sight. By the time Plover finally emerged from the drains, the war had been raging for five years straight.[5a]

was happening in Lamonic Bibber.

'The war is getting worse by the day,' squeaked Plover, 'but, oh, how lucky I am! For now I have come to this quiet and peaceful forest, where everyone lives in harmony and there is never any fighting and –'

5a The only ones not to get involved were the lions. Way up in space, they looked down on it all with their powerful telescopes and decided to leave everyone to it. On the whole they were glad they'd moved to Mars, although they wished they'd remembered to bring a few antelopes along for a snack. All they had to eat were the Martians, which tasted horrible and weren't even real. After a few years of trying to survive on the foul-tasting Non-Existent Martians, the lions all died out, so perhaps they weren't quite so super-intelligent after all.

6 The Hexagonal Pony had been born about a thousand years earlier, when a normal pony had fallen in love with a maths book. It lived in the Glass Forest[6a], along with the Giant Walking Chessmen[6b] and the Crumbs of the South.[6c]

6a The Glass Forest wasn't called the Glass Forest because it was made of glass, (although it *was* made of glass). Every tree on Earth had been made of glass since around the 8000th century, so *all* the forests of the distant future were glass forests. The Glass Forest was actually named after Charlotte Glass, the explorer who had discovered it a few hundred years before Plover was born.

6b The Giant Walking Chessmen had been created way, way back in the 751st century, when lightning had struck some normal chessmen who were having a picnic inside a giant's boot and everything had got confused because of electricity.

6c The Crumbs of the South were just some crumbs that had blown in from the South one day.

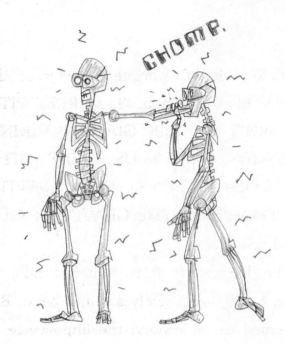

'GIANT WALKING CHESSMEN!' shouted the king of that proud people (who was actually one of the bishops). 'THIS TALKING GRAPE HAS BROUGHT US USEFUL INFORMATION! LONG HAVE WE WAITED TO VANQUISH OUR ENEMIES! LET US MARCH ON LAMONIC BIBBER AND KILL EVERYTHING IN SIGHT!'

'YES!' cried the Prime Minister of the Crumbs of the South. 'I AGREE WITH THE KING OF THE GIANT WALKING CHESSMEN! LET US RIDE THE HEXAGONAL PONY INTO BATTLE AND DANCE ON THE GRAVES OF OUR ENEMIES!'

The Hexagonal Pony couldn't talk, of course, for he was merely a dumb beast. But he seemed to understand the importance of the quest and very soon they were all heading back to town – the Giant Walking Chessmen marching, fierce and brave and true, and the Crumbs of the South riding the Hexagonal Pony and making it itch a bit, like when you've been eating biscuits in bed.

'TO WAR!' the cry went up, over and over again. 'TO WAR!'

'No!' squeaked Plover. 'I never wanted this! I only wished to live in peace! Cease this mindless bloodshed, cease it, I say!'

But it was no good. Plover watched helplessly from the sidelines as the greatest battle the world had ever known unfolded. The Crows of the Future, the Disconnected-Face-Bum-Dogs, the Pencil People, the Normal People, the evil reprogrammed Electronic Noimps with their fearsome Cannibal Skeleton Robot pilots, the Stupid Ants with Human Hands, the Hexagonal Pony, the Giant Walking Chessmen, the Crumbs of the South – all were intent on one thing and one thing only: death and destruction.

'No!' cried Plover, jumping into the middle of the fray. 'Peace! Peace! Why can't we all just get along!'

Everyone fired at him at once.

There was a little squishing sound.

And then . . .

A spark . . .

'UH OH!' shouted the king of the Cannibal Skeleton Robots, who had once been the head Fruit Scientist at the International Lord Famous Research Institute of Lamonic Bibber.' It looks like we succeeded in creating one atomic grape after all! Quick, let's –'

There was a great flash of white light.

A silence so loud it was deafening.

And then the entire world exploded.

A freezing wind blew and a hard rain fell and the wind and the rain lasted for a thousand million years.

And there were no plants on the cold, scarred ground.

No birds in the broken sky.

No fish in the roiling seas.

Another thousand million years passed.

Then another.

Then another.

Some chemicals fell down from space.

They landed on the ground, where a little town called Lamonic Bibber had once stood, between the mountains and the sea.

Yet another thousand million years went by.

And then, for the first time in millennia:

Movement.

A hand appeared amongst the rocks and stones.

A grunting noise.

Slowly a hairy figure emerged.

For a moment it simply stood there, surveying its brave new world.

Then it threw back its head and bellowed loud and clear.

'ME BACK!' cry hary figur. 'TIMM TO DO IT AL OVAH AGGEN!

'ME NATBOFF!' say Natboff.[7]

ENND

<hr />

7 'HEY! GESS WHAT? ME COME BACK AS WEL!' say voic by Natboff side. 'DISCO TO SELEBRAT?'